Wild
Justice

Wild
Justice

Richard C. Smith

St. Martin's Press
New York

Library of Congress Cataloging-in-Publication Data

Smith, Richard C. (Richard Charles)
    Wild Justice / Richard C. Smith.
        p. cm.
    ISBN 0-312-04466-6
    I. Title.
PS3569.M537918W55   1990
813'.54—dc20   89-78023

First Edition

10 9 8 7 6 5 4 3 2 1

For Thomas Spencer Smith

Wild
Justice

Revenge is a kind of wild justice;
Which the more man's nature runs to,
the more ought law to weed it out.
—Francis Bacon, *Essays: Of Revenge*

Down on
the Farm

IT WAS A HOT SUNDAY in August and we traveled down Route 15 at sixty miles per hour with the windows wide open and Bob Dylan in the tape deck. The wind and music muffled conversation, so I focused on the countryside of second-growth timber and thought about other trips I'd made to Maine, starting thirty years back when I was a five-year-old with two doting parents in a '55 Dodge touring car.

Route 15 is a broad two-lane highway cutting southeasterly over wooded hills, eventually running to the tip of Deer Isle on Penobscot Bay. We passed an occasional small town beside a lake, white clapboard houses and churches, then the road flattened out and followed the Piscataquis River through Guilford to Sangerville, our destination. It was five-thirty when we pulled into the driveway at the farmhouse, where my '69 Rambler station wagon sat in the shade of two sugar maples, looking dusty, neglected, and disreputable.

My name is Mallory, James Maxfield Mallory. I have been a private detective for about ten years now. In that time I have accumulated neither great wealth nor many possessions. Old friends, when I feel the need for luxury, are willing to share with me. A woman I know tells me it's because I'm large—six feet two, one hundred ninety-five pounds—and almost a cop, and I don't covet their wealth, so people feel safe around me.

The farmhouse belonged to two old friends, Samantha and

Jay Franklin. They'd acquired it—along with one hundred acres of hay fields, a fifty-acre woodlot, thirty-six Jersey cows, two tractors, a manure spreader, and the services of a hired hand named Hank—back in February. Before that they'd lived in a three bedroom co-op on Manhattan's Upper West Side, overlooking Central Park.

We were returning from seven days of sailing on Moosehead, a big lake that cuts thirty-five miles into the wilderness territories owned, maintained, and protected by Scott Paper Company. There are landlocked salmon in the lake that spawn in the rivers filling it, and an abundance of moose, black bear, otters, and mosquitoes. We'd brought along a good stock of exotic supplies, caught a fair number of fish, and each night—on the chosen island, after an evening swim—Jay had improvised a gourmet meal on the two-burner Coleman, while Sam and I gathered driftwood for the fire that was necessary in the cool August evenings. After dinner we talked until the fire burned down, then I'd crawl off to my sleeping bag on the padded deck of the nineteen-foot *Silhouette,* leaving Sam and Jay to the privacy of a pup tent pitched on shore.

It hadn't bothered me to sleep alone with the stars and mosquitoes that lazy summer week. Just before heading north I'd finished tracking down a pair of swindlers who'd snatched half a million dollars from my client. One of the pair had died in an ugly way, and the other was now in jail. The dead one had been a woman, and I was trying to decide whether her dying had been worth the hefty fee the client paid with such enthusiasm. It probably wasn't, but she was gone, and I didn't plan to return the fee. Now I'd had my week of soul-searching, fresh air, and sunlight, and I felt fit and reasonably at peace with my conscience.

We were back in Sangerville in time for the evening milking. Jay went out to the barn while Sam and I unloaded supplies from the Jeep 4×4. That finished, I went to Jay's office at the front of the house, with its mahogany partner's desk and matching leather chairs, blue Oriental rug, and the gold-framed portrait of Judge Rupert B. Franklin, Jay's paternal grandfather. Nine months earlier the same furniture had filled an office fifty stories above Wall Street, with a view of the planet that would have made Zeus envious.

Zeus notwithstanding, I have never envied Jay his beautiful offices, since he has to practice law in them. Occasionally I test my feelings on that subject—it's important, because if I'd stayed in law school, I'd have been guaranteed similar accommodations by the unwritten part of the Harvard diploma—but I always come up pure. I prefer my own place, on the third floor of an aging health club at the edge of Boston's dwindling red-light district, the Combat Zone.

Sitting in the outsized chair behind the desk where old Judge Franklin had written a thousand opinions of law, I used my credit card to call Boston, activated the device that plays back the messages on my machine, and listened to three recorded dial tones. The machine has limited success snaring new clients, most of whom have problems they'd prefer not to divulge to a tape recorder.

Then Michael Garrison's voice came over the line. Michael's a partner at a large Boston law firm similar to the large Wall Street firm Jay had forsaken. Michael has the odd notion that holding a telephone to his mouth is undignified, so he pushes a button on his conference speakers instead and talks through the voice-activated microphone. It gives his messages an echoing, prophetic quality.

The voice said, "Jimmy, remember Mary Wyman? You tracked down her niece six years ago. Mary's been threatened and badly beaten by unknown parties. Give me a call when you get back."

Then three more recorded dial tones, and that was it. I tried to think of all the people I knew in Boston who were mean enough to beat up a seventy-year-old woman, and all the reasons they might have for doing so. I'd have to wait for details. On a Sunday afternoon in August Michael would be out on the manicured playing fields of the Bombay Hunt Club, waving a long-handled polo mallet at seven fellow Anglophiles on horseback.

Back in the kitchen Sam sat at the big yellow table. Her blond hair was lit by the last of the sunlight coming in through the screen door behind her, putting her face in shadow. She looked cool and contented, and smiled as I came into the room. There was a cold bottle of Geary's ale opened for me, and I sat across from her with the sun in my eyes and drank half of it in one long swallow. It tasted like good beers I'd had in Ireland, the kind that never get imported to the States.

"Can you stay a few days more," Sam said, "or must you return to the land of discord?"

She talks that way because she writes romantic novels and can't always turn it off. And she's from Ireland herself, so she said it with a lilt.

"Duty calls," I told her.

"More's the pity. Jay's out with the cows and Hank. Our hired hand is stewing over our gall at taking holidays."

"Probably because he's never had one," I said. I knew the real reason for Hank's attitude was Ben Chapman, an old bachelor who owned half the town of Sangerville, the man who'd sold the farm to the Franklins. Apparently Ben had long ago promised to will the place to Hank. So Hank harbored a grudge against the new owners, which manifested itself in subtle ways, like bitching about their vacations and leaving tractors running under bedroom windows at five in the morning. He had the added charm of despising me as another interloper from the big city. But he kept working for the Franklins—jobs are scarce in northern Maine—and they weren't mean enough to fire him.

I'd met Ben Chapman back in February, when he tried to sell the Franklins a manure pile. The pile was on their land at the time, but as Ben pointed out, it hadn't been listed in the purchase and sale agreement. Jay asked him, in that case, to please remove it.

It struck me at the time that Ben looked like a man who'd just stepped out of a manure pile, which was not unusual in those parts, except that Ben's brother was a justice of the Supreme Judicial Court of Massachusetts and had taught at Harvard when Jay and I were first-year law students. Jay had been Judge Chapman's law clerk after graduation.

"Hank's gotten worse in the last few weeks," Sam said. "Frankly, I'd like to sell the cows, shut down the dairy, and be done with him. But then I think about Abby and the five girls."

I finished the Geary's and stood up. "Maybe I'll go out and help placate him."

"Be forewarned—Jay'll put you to work at the milking."

"It's been tried before." I let the screen door slam behind me and stepped out into the sunlight. The lawn and gardens in back of the house were enclosed by a short picket fence on two sides and by the long wall of the barn on the third. Beyond the fence a hay field ran uphill to woods, which were in shadow. The hillside itself was lit by the hot sun, the recently cut hay raked into lines that followed its contours. It looked like a Currier & Ives print of a summer evening in the country. I walked to the barn and stepped into the cool air of the milking room, where the thirty-six Jersey cows fed at two rows of stanchions under a low ceiling that was the floor of the big hayloft above.

It took a moment to adjust to the dim light. Hank was nowhere in sight, but Jay knelt on the cement floor beside a brown cow. Jay has a broad, sculpted face that reminds me of Picasso's portrait of Gertrude Stein, except when he smiles and looks like Chevy Chase. At that moment he frowned, trying to get the suction cups of an electric milker over the teats of the cow. The milking machine made a lot of noise and looked like a nursing extraterrestrial.

He spotted me and shouted, "Ready for work?"

"I'm just a cow observer," I shouted back. "I never touch them."

He didn't smile, but went back to the suction cups while I observed. With their brown hides and soulful eyes, Jerseys look a lot like deer. That's what I was thinking when ninety pounds of tightly baled hay dropped out of the ceiling directly above my head. I jerked back so it hit me on the shoulder instead of breaking my neck, but the impact knocked me onto the cement floor. Hank appeared at the edge of the trapdoor in the ceiling.

"You idiot!" he shouted.

I almost laughed at him. He jumped from the loft and landed a few paces away as I got to my feet. I brushed sawdust from my jeans, then glanced up and recognized the look in his eyes—the look of a man who wants to bust heads and doesn't need much provocation to start. He was a giant, at least five inches taller and fifty pounds heavier than I. I barely had time to wonder what the hell was wrong with the guy when he drew back his right fist for a barroom punch, I stepped into it, took it back farther than he'd intended, twisting the arm in one quick motion, then walking him up against the wall. He hit hard enough to shake dust out of the loft overhead. Jay switched off the electric pump and shouted, "Hank!"

I think it was the sudden silencing of the pump that stopped him. I felt his muscles relax and I let him loose, taking two quick steps back. He turned and glared at me, said "Shit," and hauled off and kicked the fallen bale of hay. Then he pushed past and stalked to the open door in back and went on out. I rubbed my neck and looked at Jay.

"A little unresolved hostility, or was I standing where only a city slicker would stand?"

"You were standing just fine. You okay?"

I brushed off more sawdust and said, "I'm dirty."

We looked at each other and suddenly both laughed. "Reminds me of that night at the Dugout when the big Irishman got mad at you for playing Frank Sinatra on the jukebox," Jay said. Then he frowned, losing the Chevy Chase look. "It's because of Ben Chapman. Ben got himself killed this afternoon, cutting wood. Pulled a tree on his head with a tractor."

"You're kidding."

"Sounds stupid, doesn't it? Hank heard about it on the CB scanner, got real upset, and I told him to go home to his family. But Hank has never gone home in the middle of milking, so he stayed. I'm sorry, Jimmy. We'd better finish here and go in and tell Sam. This could be the last straw as far as Hank's working here."

"No pun intended, I hope." He smiled again, and I volunteered to help—I'd had some rudimentary instruction on milking machines during my visit in February. Working together, it took us only about twice as long as it should have to finish milking and then clean the equipment. On the way back to the house I smelled coals burning in the barbecue, a nice summer smell. In the kitchen we found Hank's wife, Abby, at the table with Sam.

"Abby just told me what happened," Sam said.

"I came to apologize for Hank," she said with a gruff voice, keeping her eyes on Jay. "Are you hurt, Mr. Mallory?"

"I'm fine. It was an accident."

"Getting mad was no accident, but he's terrible upset about old Ben. That's no excuse, but maybe it's enough so you'll turn a blind eye this once, Jay. If Hank lost his job, it'd kill him."

"Never mind, Abby. It's all right."

"I just wanted to apologize," she said again. Having got what she came for, she stood up from the table and went to the front door, her head bowed.

Jay met her at the door and put his hand on her shoulder. "It's okay," he said. She smiled up at him, then back at Sam and me, and went out.

Jay closed the door and said, "Shit."

Sam shook her head sadly. "Poor Ben." Then she looked at me and said, "You're a mess."

So I went upstairs to wash, and stopped in the guest room to change into a clean pair of jeans and a fresh T-shirt. Back downstairs half an hour later Sam was alone again in the kitchen, at the counter opening the three Styrofoam packs of porterhouse steaks we'd picked up before leaving Greenville.

"I can't believe Hank attacked you like that," she said as soon as I came into the room.

I went to the counter and pulled the cork from a bottle of red wine Sam had set out beside the sink. "People are funny," I told her. "He needed a target, and I was available. Why do you think he took Ben's death so hard?"

"Ben was like a father to Hank, or used to be before they fought. Your father dies when you're still angry with him, you feel a lot of guilt. I know about that."

"Ben didn't strike me as the fatherly type."

She shrugged, putting the last of the steaks on the platter. I got wineglasses out and poured us each a glass. We stood looking out the window over the sink, thinking about Hank's behavior. It didn't make any sense to me, but I decided not to worry about it. I was on vacation. Sam turned on the tap and washed her hands, then looked up at me and said, "I'd better take a look at the garden—it's probably overrun with killer vegetables after a week without my attentions. Jay's upstairs changing. Would you throw the steaks on the grill?"

She took a wicker basket along with her. I got the steaks and my glass of wine and took everything out to the grill. The coals had burned down nicely, and I stood with my wine and the view of the hay fields and waited for the meat to char while the light faded and dew settled in the grass. Sam came from the garden with half a dozen yellow squash and gave me a rueful smile going past. "Full of weeds."

Jay came out to join me, bringing the bottle of wine. He sat on the steps and looked up at the hay field and the beginning of the sunset. "Nice to be in the country," he said. I swatted an imaginary mosquito and he smiled. When the steaks were done, we brought them in on the platter. Sam had set the table with blue cloth napkins, blue china, and the good silver. "Tonight we eat civilized," she said.

But what had been meant as a party turned out to be a wake for Ben Chapman. They told me stories about him, like the time a cagey tourist offered to buy "a hundred dollars worth of land," and Ben brought him a wheelbarrow full of dirt. And the time Ben clobbered a hunter up from Boston who'd shot Ben's goat, thinking it was a deer, and the story got into *The New York Times*. Sam said, "We should call the Judge."

"He's probably on his way up," Jay said. "We'll see him at the funeral."

I took a bite of steak and finished a glass of wine. The sun had gone down and it was getting dark in the room. "Do you think Ben might have left Hank a few acres after all?" I said.

"I'm pretty sure he died intestate," Jay answered me. "He once asked me to draft a will, then changed his mind when I told him what my fee would be. Since the Judge was his only family, he didn't really need one."

"This isn't much of a send-off for you, James," Sam said. "Did he tell you, Jay, he has to leave tomorrow?"

"Urgent business in Boston."

"If you stay," Sam said, "we could go back up to the lake for another week." She said it with such a wistful note I was tempted to say I would stay. I thought a bit about the sail we'd just finished. The wind had been light out of the northwest most of the day, and we'd flown the blue spinnaker from the old spa at Kineo all the way down to Greenville, almost twenty miles. The sun had been hot, the trees lit up green, the sky blue and marked only by the high vapor trails of jets heading back from Europe to New York and Boston.

That's when the front door burst open and Judy, Hank's fifteen-year-old, ran into the kitchen sobbing.

It took us a few minutes to calm her down and learn the fact she'd come to communicate. The police had arrested Hank. They were charging him with Ben Chapman's murder.

CHAPTER TWO

Until the
Cows Come Home

IT WAS AFTER TEN when Jay and I reached the county seat at Dover-Foxcroft where they were holding Hank. Dover-Foxcroft's the local commercial center, with a population of at least three thousand. There was a shopping center at its western border, then a hospital complex—a wooden Victorian building with a newer, brick structure beside it. The little business district had a five & dime, a bank, a real estate office, and a print shop. The only commercial enterprises open for business at that hour were a Coke machine and a Pepsi machine standing together on the sidewalk outside the five & dime.

The courthouse and jail were at the far end of town. The jail had a tiny exercise yard, a basketball hoop against the wall of the building, and a chain fence with razor wire at the top. We went into the county sheriff's office where an old cop with a bald head and cynical grin sat with his feet up, drinking from a Styrofoam cup of coffee. He was expecting us. He nodded at Jay and got to his feet.

"Let's go up and see the D.A. He's all excited about having an honest-to-God premeditated murder to prosecute. Who's your friend?"

"Jim Mallory," I said.

"Detective Patrick Cross." He put out his hand to shake as we started up the stairs. "You a lawyer?"

"Private investigator, from Boston."

"Well, well, it's an honor." I couldn't see his face, but the tone of voice was sarcastic. Upstairs we crossed a hall to an office where Gary McGuire, county prosecutor, sat at a green metal desk, smoking a little cigar that smelled like burned cloves. He was a short, black-haired, thick-chested guy in shirt sleeves and tie. It had surprised me that the D.A. would be there on a Sunday night, and it surprised me more when I saw the suit, tie, and freshly pressed shirt. As Cross introduced us McGuire gave me a smug and confident smile, like a law student who'd just been asked a question he could answer. Cross winked at me and said, "Mallory's private talent, up from Boston."

The look of confidence faded a little. "Private what?"

"Investigator," I told him.

He stubbed out his cigar and said, "Let's see your license." He took a full minute to copy my name and address onto a yellow legal pad, then handed back the license and turned to Jay. "You representing Hank?"

"Abby asked me to see him. What have you got?"

"I'll put you down as counsel of record," he said, and wrote that on the pad. When he looked up he hardened his voice and said, "I'll tell you up front, you may be a big-shot Wall Street lawyer, but I've got an open-and-shut case against Hank. Don't give me any bullshit. Tell him what we got, Pat."

It didn't surprise me that McGuire knew all about Jay's previous affiliation. There are only about ten practicing lawyers in Piscataquis County.

Cross finished his coffee, grinned at me, and missed the gray metal wastebasket with the empty cup. "You know Clive Linscott, Jay," then added for my benefit, "owns a big chunk of land in this town and runs a trap line on it, for fox and fisher cat. He found Ben's body in a woodlot off Parkman Road at three forty-five this afternoon. Judge Chapman was up from Boston for the weekend, staying at Ben's place, so we know Ben finished lunch and went out to cut at one o'clock exactly.

"That fixes the time of death pretty close. Medical examiner says probably three o'clock. Ben had his head stove in by a tree that'd fallen onto his tractor. It was set up to look like an accident."

"How so?" Jay said.

"You two probably don't know much about cuttin' timber, being from the city. But when you fell a tree with a chain saw, you start with one horizontal cut on the side where you want it to drop, then come in at a diagonal from the back." He made chopping motions with his hands to demonstrate. "If you cut too deep on the horizontal"—he sliced with his left—"the tree leans onto your saw blade, and sometimes it gets stuck like that. Then you might need to pull the tree down with a drag chain. Things were set up to make it look like Ben had done just that—chain running from the tree to the tractor, Ben up in the driver's seat. But the chain was too short."

"So the tree fell on his head," I said.

"Exactly," Cross said, his tone implying he appreciated my sagacity. "Only an idiot or a drunk would make a mistake like that, and Ben wasn't either. So I took a close look at the stump. It'd been cut at a diagonal in back, by a chain saw. Somebody set up that scene with the drag chain, then dropped the tree on Ben. Our expert was in this evening—he says the prints on the diagonal cut don't match Ben's saw."

"Chain saws make prints?" I said.

"Sure. Like identifying a typewriter. Nicks in the chain leave a pattern in the wood—we've used it to track illegal timbering. You probably don't get much of that in Boston."

"The prints aren't reliable," Jay said.

"They are when you've got a good clean cut, and that's

what we got here. Medical examiner found a big bruise on the back of Ben's neck. I'd say he was out cold when the tree hit him. I figure Hank knocked him out, sat him in the tractor, then dropped the tree on him. Hank's good enough in the woods to manage that."

"Why Hank?"

"You know about them falling out over Ben's will," McGuire said. He lit a new cigar.

"That's not probable cause for arrest," Jay told him.

Cross said, "It's motive, Jay. Anyway, we asked the expert to match Hank's saw with the prints on that stump. It was Hank's saw that dropped the tree on Ben."

Jay looked at McGuire and said, "How'd you get the saw?"

"It was a legal search incident to a valid arrest," McGuire said.

"Besides, we asked Hank for permission," Cross pointed out. "We live by the Constitution in Dover-Foxcroft."

"If Hank wanted to kill Ben," I said, "why'd he use his own saw?"

"He couldn't use Ben's saw, because as part of the scene he'd bound that one in the deep horizontal cut, like I explained. He used his own saw to make the diagonal cut, probably not knowing about chain-saw prints. Not many people do."

"How could he expect you to miss the obvious fact that the tree had been cut?" Jay said. "It doesn't make sense."

McGuire put in his two cents. "Hank's no brain surgeon. There's insanity in his family."

"What does Hank say?"

"That's the clincher, Jay," Cross answered before McGuire had a chance to speak. "Says he was out back of your place cutting between noon and four, and had the saw with him the whole time. Even after we told him about the prints and the time of death, he stuck to the same story—which ain't really a story, just a dumb lie."

Cross stood abruptly and said, "Why don't I take you down to see him? If that's all right with Mr. McGuire?" Once again, his tone of voice was sarcastic.

McGuire didn't catch the sarcasm, just nodded, then said to me, "If you plan to do any work on this case, you come in and fill out the proper registration forms tomorrow morning." It was too late in the evening to badger a small-town D.A., so I told him I'd be sure to do that, with just enough lack of conviction to let him know he had a rebel on his hands. Then Jay and I got up to follow Cross out of the room.

The air in the corridor smelled fresh after the cigar stink in the little office. Cross said, "Don't bother about those forms, they aren't necessary. D.A.'s a part-time job in this county, it don't pay much so we don't get too many hotshots. I'd do the job myself, save everybody a lot of trouble, but the law says you need a degree." It was an odd statement to make to a complete stranger. Cross apparently had something in common with Hank—another disgruntled man working for somebody he considered his superior by privilege only.

He led us down a different stairway and through a heavy door into the jail, then left us in an interrogation room and went back to the cell block for Hank. When he reappeared he had one hand on Hank's elbow, smiling as if he were leading him to a surprise birthday party. He left us alone, closing the door as he went out.

Hank wore a bright-orange, long-sleeved coverall that was probably meant to make him look conspicuous in a crowd—if he ever escaped and could find a crowd in Dover-Foxcroft big enough to hide in. He stayed upright, against the wall across the table from where I stood. He stared defiantly at Jay, who'd settled into a chair at the far end of the room. Jay sat there looking back at him, as if trying to decide how to start.

Hank said, "What you doing here?"

"I'm your lawyer, if you'll have me."

"I don't need no lawyer. I was in the back woods cuttin' firewood all day with that saw, until the cows come in for milking at five. You know that, I get to cut out back if I give you half the wood, which I think sucks. I do all the work and you get half, just because you own the fucking land."

Jay shook his head and said quietly, "This isn't the time to tell me what you think of me, Hank. Were you alone all afternoon?"

"What do you think? Course I was."

"Did you come in for lunch?"

"Abby packs me lunch every day and I eat in the woods. I left the saw out there when I come in at five. In summer, I cut after I finish milking, 'cause the light's still good. Tonight I went back out and took the saw home right after work." He shot me a nasty look but didn't make any reference to the fight in the barn that had interrupted his normal schedule.

"Somebody coulda borrowed it during that time I was milking," he said.

"Doesn't work, Hank. Ben was killed at three o'clock."

"I didn't do it."

"Tell me why you were so upset this afternoon. Convince me it wasn't because you'd just come from killing Ben."

"Ben and I had our differences, but he promised to make it right about the land he stole from me—then he went and died. You'd be pissed too. But I didn't kill him."

"He couldn't make it right about the farm, Hank."

"Not the farm. There was other land the county took for taxes when my daddy got killed. Ben bought it at auction when I was a kid, said he was holdin' it for me. I found out he'd lied, but when I went to him about it, he said he'd make it right."

"Did you tell McGuire that?"

"No."

"Don't tell him. Tomorrow they'll bring you before a judge to bind you over. I'll be there. The state'll pay my fees."

"Fuck that," Hank said, then looked over at me. For just a second he didn't look mean, he looked scared.

"You need a lawyer, Hank."

"I'll take care of myself." He lifted his head and said distinctly, "There's things to be taken care of." Then he walked to the door and went out into the corridor. Nobody was waiting to collect him, so he turned left and disappeared from sight.

Jay looked at me and shrugged tiredly. He got up from the table and we went back to the sheriff's office, where Cross sat reading a magazine called *Guns and Ammo,* drinking another cup of coffee.

He said, "Hank convince you of his innocence, Jay?"

Jay ignored the question and picked up the phone at the desk. I said, "Unless you've got someone else on duty, your prisoner's wandering through the corridors without a watchdog."

"Thanks for reminding me," Cross said, and got up slowly to go off in the direction we'd come from. Security wasn't very tight at the Piscataquis County Jail. Jay must have called the farmhouse, because I heard him speak with Sam, then ask for Abby.

I wandered back in the direction of the cell block and found Cross locking the grilled door at the end of the block. Everything in that part of the jail was painted a dingy yellow. I could see Hank lying on a cot in a cell—the door of the cell itself was open. Cross saw me notice that and said, "Ain't like he can get through this door, so why give him claustrophobia? He's just a farm boy."

I looked at him closely to see if he was serious, and he said, "You're thinking I've been a cop too long and gettin' lax, that it?" I didn't say anything, and he started back along the corridor. I followed.

"Truth is," he said back at me, "I don't blame Hank for killin' Ben, and I see no reason to make things worse for him."

"What'd you have against Ben?"

He kept walking but said over his shoulder, "He was a taker."

"He ever take from you?"

Cross stopped and faced me. "Once or twice, but that was long ago. Thing is, Ben owned a lot of land in these parts, and sometimes he skirted real close to breaking the law in order to get more of it. Nothing a dumb cop could do anything about. The few times he stepped over the line, his brother, the Judge, came up from Boston and fixed things with the D.A."

"Was it land Ben took from you?"

"That wasn't my complaint." He gave me the cynical smile again. "He took my wife. For a little while, anyway."

Then he went on into the office, picked up his cup of coffee, took it to a little sink and refrigerator unit in one corner of the room and dumped it. He kept his eyes on me, reached into a cabinet over the sink for a pint bottle of Seagrams, and poured a few inches into the cup. He lifted it in a toast. "For my liver," he said.

Jay hung up, looked at Cross, then back at me. "That's it for tonight." He told Cross he'd see him in court the next day, and we stepped back out into the cool night air. As we walked across the macadam, I smelled woodsmoke coming from one of the neighboring houses.

When we were in the car I said, "You okay?"

Jay turned the key in the ignition, leaned back and sighed.

"I'm sick of trying to get the truth out of people who end up in that crummy interrogation room. Especially when they're guilty as hell."

"You've only been doing it six months," I pointed out.

He smiled at that and said, "Sorry. Guess I'm just tired because it's past my bedtime. What was that little exchange between you and Cross, just before we left?"

"He was telling me he had a motive for killing Ben Chapman." I repeated our conversation in the corridor.

"That's just Cross," he said. "Likes to stir things up. Forty years wasted on a hick police force have made him bitter. He's too smart for his own good."

"Why'd he stay in Dover-Foxcroft?"

"He was born here."

I didn't point out that lots of people, myself included, had been born in small towns. I said, "What did the D.A. mean about insanity in Hank's family?"

"Hank's mom shot and killed his dad when Hank was twelve. They put her in the state hospital in Bangor. She slit her wrists with a broken Coke bottle and bled to death a couple of hours after they admitted her. That's when Ben took Hank in to live at the farm."

"Poor Hank."

"No kidding. Maybe that's why I feel for him, despite everything. The fact that he can function at all is amazing. Makes me think I've grown up on a bed of roses."

"Your folks' place in the city isn't exactly a flophouse," I said. "Is there a bar open at this hour?"

"The Red Oak gets rowdy this time of night. Let's go back to the house."

Half an hour later we were back in the farmhouse. Sam was asleep on one of the couches in the living room. She'd built a fire, and we threw more wood on the coals without waking her or turning on lights. I went up to my room and got a bottle of Courvoisier I'd been saving as a parting gift.

We drank quietly, watching the fire burn down to embers. Out through the front windows, between the tops of the two big maples, I could see a billion stars. I thought about Abby and her children down in the hand-built shack at the far side of the front field, and about Judy running across the field to tell us about her father. I wondered what would happen to them.

Then I thought about Boston. I looked forward to getting home.

could have killed Ben in a fit of anger, then made a hasty attempt to cover it up. But that doesn't fit either—Cross said Ben was still alive when the tree hit him."

"What if the killer switched saws with Hank at some point, used Hank's saw to cut down the tree, then switched them back while Hank was in doing the milking?"

"Couldn't happen. Hank's saw was salvaged from the dump—you couldn't duplicate the look of it any more than you could fake his fingerprints. He'd have known."

"Then Hank's lying," I said. "Either he killed Ben, or somebody else did, and he's lying to protect the somebody else."

"There isn't anybody he'd do that for. He's got no family except Abby and the girls, no close friends."

"And Abby didn't drop a tree on Ben."

"Right. Maybe it's Cross who's lying. He could be setting Hank up for some reason." All of a sudden Jay gave a short, unhappy laugh. "We sound like a couple of first-year law students, trying to guess the rationale behind the rule in Shelley's case—maybe this, maybe that."

"Why don't I at least talk to the guy who found the body and take a look at that woodlot?"

"What about your urgent business?"

"A few hours won't hurt. I'll call Boston."

"I'd appreciate it, Jimmy. I've got a feeling this is going to turn into a mess, and I'll need all the help I can get. Come up with some magic for me."

"I'll try. I owe you one. Or you owe me one, or something like that. I'll take a look around."

An hour later I drove the Rambler down a narrow gravel road, throwing up a cloud of dust and pebbles, thinking I was doing what a professional should never do—getting involved in a case without committing myself to follow through to the end. But that's what friends are for.

Jay had called Linscott, the old trapper who'd found Ben's body, and he'd agreed to meet me on Parkman Road at the start of the trail leading into the woodlot where Ben had died. Before heading out I'd taken a look at Jay's survey map of Sangerville. Parkman Road was a long, winding dead end, with only a few rectangular blots on the map to show houses. Ben's house had been built after the map was printed, but Jay marked it for me, where Chapman Pond and the gravel road intersected and the contour lines showed a low, rounded hill. The only other residence close to that end of the road was Clive Linscott's farm.

According to Jay, Clive was another old bachelor who, like Ben, owned more real estate than he'd ever need. He spent most of his time wandering his thousand acres, tending trap lines. The thousand acres impressed me, but when I asked Jay how much all that property was worth he'd said, "Probably three hundred an acre, if you could find a buyer. And you couldn't. Might be worth a great deal someday, but I doubt it. People from Boston come up here and don't realize property values are different. A partnership came into Bangor and converted a parking garage into luxury condominiums. The bank foreclosed, and it's still trying to sell them. If you want a penthouse apartment with a view across Kenduskeag Stream to the Penobscot County Jail, I know where you can pick one up for a song." It reminded me of the old saying: What three factors affect the value of real estate? Location, location, location.

Coming over the crest of a small hill I spotted a gray-haired man blocking the road ahead, a rifle held at rest under one arm. He pointed into the woods, and I pulled the Rambler to the side and parked in the heavy underbrush. I got out and said, "Clive Linscott?"

"Right."

Linscott was a rangy old guy, weathered face shaded by a battered Red Sox cap. He wore a red checked flannel shirt, torn at the top buttonhole, and faded khakis over boots that looked like they'd been seasoned in cow manure. Probably in his sixties, about five nine and not heavy, he looked mean and tough as a goat. The rifle was a World War II carbine, big enough to kill a moose.

"What's the gun for?" I said.

"We might come on a deer," he said without showing any expression, "or we might come on Hank Tuttle and get us a reward. Franklin said you wanted to see where Ben got killed. Come along, then." And he started up the trail.

I followed and said to his back, "It's not hunting season."

"You ain't a game warden."

I had to agree with him there. We were silent for another hundred yards, but I wanted to get him talking, so I said, "Nice weather."

"Too dry," he said. "When the rain comes, it'll wash out the crops."

"What have you got for crops?"

"Ain't got no crops."

I decided to relax and enjoy the walk and the dry weather. The old trail was grassy and moss-covered and wide enough for a car. There were young birch and maples growing thick on both sides, with an occasional old spruce that had been spared by the loggers who'd clear-cut that part of the state thirty years earlier. The trees they'd spared all had some twist or deformity that made them useless for timber, and I wondered how many of the new seedling evergreens would inherit that survival mechanism. Only the good die young.

About five hundred yards from where I'd left the Rambler we passed through a gate in an old stone wall and came into a stand of bigger maples that looked as if they'd been tended. The woodlot was a hundred yards farther in. Ben's red tractor was parked in the center, half obscured by the branches of the tree that had killed him. The leaves on the killer tree were still green, just starting to wilt in the hot sun. Around the perimeter of the clearing other trees had been dropped into the woods; there were raw stumps everywhere, and stacks of cordwood. The only sound was the buzz of insects in the underbrush. It looked ominous and threatening, as only the deep forest can look when you let your imagination dwell on the isolation, and I wondered what it must have been like to come into that clearing when there was a dead man sitting up on the tractor.

I said to Linscott, "How did you happen to find him?"

"I heard the chain saw and come to investigate. This land belongs to me. Ben was stealing my timber."

That surprised me—another local volunteering a motive for murdering Ben? I said, "He must have been working here for weeks."

"Yesterday was the first I heard him. Sound travels funny 'cross these woods, sometimes you can't pinpoint it. There are places you can stand on flat ground, give a shout, and raise an echo like you was facin' a rock wall a hundred feet high." He went over to the tractor and leaned against it, watching me.

I thought it unlikely that Clive Linscott ever gave a shout in the woods just to hear his echo. I left him standing at the tractor and made the circuit of the clearing, stopping to examine the stump—it looked as if it'd been cut clear through with a saw. I didn't find any clues. I walked around the spreading branches and back to Linscott at the tractor.

"Is everything the way you found it yesterday?"

"The body's gone, and they cut off the base of that tree, took it in for evidence." He pointed at the stump.

"Cross says you found him at three forty-five."

"That's when I got back to the house to call. I live pretty close, ten minutes through the woods."

"Don't suppose you saw anybody else in the woods?"

"Nope."

"How far is it from here to the Franklins' farm?"

"Not far. Half a mile that way. Their border runs with mine. Hank coulda walked it in ten minutes."

I looked in the direction of the Franklins' farm and tried to imagine Hank stalking away from the scene of the murder, just as he'd stalked away from the barn the day before.

Linscott's body tensed. He stepped from the tractor and pointed the carbine back at the trail. I turned that way and froze.

I suppose I'd expected Hank, lurking at the edge of the clearing, returning to the scene of the crime. Instead I saw an attractive young woman dressed as if for a stroll through Boston Common. She wore a tailored blue business suit, pinstriped white cotton blouse with a Ralph Lauren polo pony on the lapel, and blue and white Reeboks over nylons. She had long blond hair parted in the middle and a nice smile she sent uncertainly across the twenty yards of brush and loose slashings. She carried a briefcase.

"Don't shoot," she said.

CHAPTER FOUR

Back to Boston

HER FACE WAS EXPRESSIVE and pretty, and she had what's called an English complexion. In another age her grandmother might have worn white dresses and carried a parasol through Green Park in London. She was very young, maybe twenty-five. Linscott was still pointing the gun at her, and I reached to push the muzzle to the ground. He resisted at first, then relaxed his grip on the stock. With the gun up he'd looked intense and dangerous, and when he spoke the words came out with an energy that contrasted with his previous noncommittal drawl.

"Who are you?" he said. "What you want?"

She came across the intervening twenty yards of brush and said mildly, "You ought to be more careful with that thing. I'm Dana McOscar."

"The professor's daughter?"

"That's right. All grown up, Mr. Linscott." She smiled. She was, in fact, taller than Linscott. Her eyes—blue, with high-lights of amber—were almost level with mine. She gave me an appraising look and said, "I saw your car. I'm Judge Chapman's law clerk."

I wondered what a law clerk was doing in the deep woods. "My name is Mallory," I said.

"I know. McGuire told me. He drove me in from the airport this morning." She looked again at Linscott, he said with a grunt,

"I'm going," and headed for the woods. We watched him go out of sight behind the trees.

Dana said, "Why do you think he was so quick with that gun? He looked like he'd seen a ghost."

"He thought you were Hank Tuttle or a deer," I told her.

"How do you know him?"

"I used to spend summer vacations in Sangerville, when my father taught at the university. Mr. Linscott chased me off his land more than once—thought I was springing traps to save the animals." She smiled and looked in the direction he had taken. "He was right too," she said.

I looked again at the business suit, the nylons, and briefcase. "What are you doing here?" I said.

She returned the appraising look, ignored the question, and said my name, "James Maxfield Mallory," rolling it out like a phrase from Berlitz. "I saw the car with Massachusetts plates. It's a classic, by the way—vintage 1969, isn't it? I had one like it when I was sixteen. McGuire told me you were from Massachusetts—working with Jay Franklin to get Hank out of trouble. He told me a lot about you. A Detective Cross called an old crony in Boston last night to get the scoop. Apparently you're 'tenacious and competent,' which doesn't make McGuire happy. He made a pass at me, by the way, at seven-thirty in the morning—which I thought was enterprising."

I wondered if the chatter was from nervousness or habit. "If you won't tell me what you're doing here, at least explain the briefcase."

She smiled, said, "I use it to conceal a gun," and reached in to pull out a nasty-looking .38.

I think she expected me to register shock, because she looked disappointed when all I said was, "Lots of guns around here."

"It's a woman's best friend. I'm licensed to carry, which means I'm trained to use it." She put the gun back in the briefcase.

"I don't like handguns," I said. "Too noisy."

"Must make your job difficult. I'm out here in the woods because I wanted to talk with you. Walk me back to the road?"

I took one last look at the tractor and the bloodied tree limb that had killed Ben Chapman. Then I bowed slightly and pointed to the trail. "Carry your bag?"

She smiled again and led the way, keeping the bag. It was a nice smile. She was tall enough so her stride matched mine. About twenty yards into the woods she surprised me by saying, "I think Hank's innocent."

"Didn't McGuire tell you about his iron-clad evidence?"

"Sure. There's got to be some explanation."

"Why?"

"Why some explanation, or why do I care? When I was a kid Hank was my hero. He knew how to cut trees, fix tractors, milk cows. He's not a killer."

"Being competent doesn't disqualify you from murder. Sometimes it helps. When was the last time you saw Hank?"

"People don't change that much," she told me, once again ignoring my question but responding to the underlying thought. Her saying that about people made me remember how young she was. She glanced behind us. "Funny how scary the woods are sometimes."

"Does the Judge agree with you?" I asked, and when she gave me a puzzled look I added, "That Hank's innocent?"

"I haven't asked him."

"How's he taking all this?"

"He's a widower and hasn't any kids, so Ben was his last family—his last real tie to this town too."

"Except now he owns half of it."

She gave me a sideways glance with the blue eyes. "I guess that's true. Most of it was family land, going back generations. Ben was oldest son, so he inherited. They're very old-fashioned people." She was silent for another dozen yards. "The Judge has a bad heart. I wish he hadn't been up here when it happened."

"Being in Boston wouldn't have made it easier."

"Oh, yes, it would have," she said with absolute certainty. We came out to the road.

"Let's walk," she said. "It's not far and I need the exercise."

"And it's a nice day to walk." There was a hot breeze blowing through the branches overhead, and the underbrush on each side of Parkman Road was dry and dusty. We passed a raspberry bush full of ripe fruit, and I stopped to pick a handful, half of which I passed to Dana. We walked along eating the fruit.

"Unless Hank is lying to protect somebody," I said, "it doesn't look good for him."

"There's something horrible about killing a man who's unconscious," she answered me. "Leaves them so unprepared for . . . whatever. McGuire told me Ben was unconscious when the tree hit him. That would take someone like Linscott, mean enough to trap small animals and club them to death. Not someone gentle like Hank."

I couldn't help smiling at that. She noticed and said, "You don't know him." We'd come to a fork in the road where a driveway cut into the woods to the right. I knew from Jay's map it led up to Clive Linscott's farm. I heard a car and took Dana a step to the side. A black Mercedes topped the hill behind us, coming faster than I would have expected. The sun on the windshield hid the driver's face. He was pushing the car at sixty on the narrow road. I just barely saw his rear wheels spin as he took the next bend in a cloud of dust. Dana said, "Asshole," with a flash of anger that seemed to make her happy.

"Must be headed for Ben's," I said.

"The Judge isn't expecting visitors."

"Let's see."

Ben's place was around the next bend, on a rise of ground overlooking Chapman Pond. The house was tiny and boxlike, with small windows set in vinyl siding, square and ugly as a New Jersey tract house. It faced the pond, but its view of the water would be obscured by the beech trees growing up the slope from the shore.

There was no black Mercedes in the driveway, only a red Fiat sports car, the Judge's, and a pickup truck that had been Ben's.

We stopped at the foot of the hill and Dana said, "Will you be staying in town?"

"I'm leaving for Boston this afternoon."

"What about Hank?"

"I don't know. Can you think of something I could do to help him?"

She thought a moment, then shrugged. "I'll work on it. Good-bye then." She reached to shake hands. I held her hand a second longer than necessary, but it wasn't meant to be flirtatious, it was an involuntary gesture—I had the feeling she still had something to say to me. But she took her hand away and started up the hill.

I went looking for the black Mercedes. The road ahead ended at a wooden gate blocking a driveway that ran into the woods. I remembered seeing the driveway on Jay's map, but he'd said nobody lived up there.

I turned back. It had been curiosity that brought me that far, and I didn't have time to waste trespassing on some rich person's private property if the only point was to tell him he was a jerk for driving sixty miles an hour on a narrow country road. I suppose if you own a Mercedes you have to do that once in a while, just to get your money's worth. I left it at that.

Back at the Franklins' there was a very different vehicle parked under the trees, a beat-up yellow pickup truck. It was rust-eaten and the bumpers had been replaced by two-by-fours bolted to the frame. It made my Rambler look, by comparison, almost flashy.

The house was quiet, which meant Jay and Sam were hard at work in their respective offices. I used my credit card to call Michael Garrison from the kitchen. His secretary, the lovely Ms. Penny Giles, answered on the first ring. She always talks a little too loud, as if she's trying to deliver a message through a bad connection. She once told me it's a habit she picked up from thirty-five years of trying to communicate with self-centered bosses. She excludes Michael from that category—she thinks he can leap tall buildings in a single bound and squeeze coal into diamonds.

"He's at a closing, Jimmy. He said if you called I should tell you Mary Wyman will meet you at your office at five tonight. Michael wants to meet with you after that."

"Any idea what's going on?"

"Not at all. Can you make that schedule?"

"Sure. Tell him he'll have to buy me a drink. At the Parker House, downstairs, six-thirty. Okay?"

"Okay. He said to remind you Mary Wyman's eccentric."

"I'll keep that in mind."

When I hung up it was after eleven and the pickup truck was gone, so I took two cold Geary's from the fridge and carried them in to Jay's office. He sat at the big desk tapping a pencil on the green felt blotter. He said, "It's early for beer," but took the bottle gratefully and drank half of it in one swallow.

"That guy who just left," he said, wiping his mouth with the back of his hand, "killed two kids, driving drunk. Now he's out on bail, driving without a license, and wants to hire me because his present lawyer's incompetent. Which is probably true—at least I hope so. That's the kind of client I get these days."

"Make you wish you were back in Manhattan?"

He snorted. "White-collar executives drive drunk and kill kids too. How'd it go with Linscott?"

"I met a beautiful woman."

I told him about it while we finished the beers. As he listened some of the worry left his face, and he gave me the Chevy Chase grin. "I met Dana once," he said, "in the Judge's chambers. She's beautiful in an exotic sort of way. And very young. How come you're always falling for lawyers?"

"It's probably a yearning after my unfulfilled destiny—and I didn't fall for her. But she thinks Hank's innocent. She knew him when she was a kid."

"I'll give her credit for that. You come up with anything?"

"Nothing concrete. Linscott's an odd duck. How much do you know about him?"

"Just what I told you this morning. He's an old Mainer, probably never been out of the state—just like Ben. The two of them were the town's womanizers, I'm told, twenty years ago. But I doubt Linscott or anyone else killed Ben over a woman."

"Linscott claims he owns the property Ben was cutting on."

"Could be true. Title records up here are screwy. Too many borders marked by trees and stone walls that disappeared years ago. But people don't kill each other over cordwood, they hire lawyers and go to court. I understand Linscott does quite a bit of that."

"What do you think about Detective Cross?"

"I've tried to figure some reason why he'd set up Hank, but I can't."

"Then we come back to Hank lying to protect someone. Think Abby knows where he's hiding? It would help if you could talk with him."

"She might know, but Hank would never go along with it. But I'll try."

I told him about our run-in with the black Mercedes.

"There's a big old farm back there, up on a hill with beautiful views. Used to belong to a hippie who lived up here summers and sold antiques in Florida winters. Guy from Massachusetts bought it last spring, had dreams of living off the land, like Thoreau. I represented him at the closing. He came into town anxious to learn all the local history, then got bored and went back to the city. The Mercedes must be his."

"That's all I came up with," I said. "Not exactly magic."

"You did what there was to do, Jimmy. I appreciate it."

By then it was almost noon. I went up to pack, and when I came back down Sam was with Jay in the kitchen, making a pot of coffee. I got my two-quart Thermos from the car and filled it.

"Jay says you met a beautiful woman in the woods," Sam said.

"An exotically beautiful woman."

"You're such a charmer." She smiled. "I'm going to make you into a character in my latest book, then I won't miss you so much." She kissed me on the cheek.

I smiled, shook hands with Jay. "Good luck. Keep me posted." Then I was off.

The first segment of the drive back to Boston is secondary roads out to the turnpike. It was flat farming country, fields of corn and potatoes, with an occasional herd of cows. It took an hour to get to Route 95.

Once out on the open road I poured coffee from the Thermos and set the steaming cup on the dash. As I drove I thought about the week of good times on the lake and then the sudden mess with Hank. Part of me felt guilty for leaving while things were unresolved, but I didn't think my staying would help. And for the moment, it wasn't my problem. I had Mary Wyman to think about.

It didn't seem like four hours had passed when I came into Boston over the Mystic Tobin Bridge. Small boats in the harbor way below left trailing wakes, and I could look out and see jets taking off from Logan. The skyline was thick with new buildings, and after a week in the country it all looked like a miracle of progress and human endeavor.

CHAPTER FIVE

The Cat Lady

I DROVE DIRECTLY to the Trojan Gym and Health Club, just off Stuart Street at the edge of the so-called Combat Zone, a stone's throw from Beacon Hill and the Public Garden. I parked the Rambler in its place in the back alley between the club and the old Bradford Hotel, and took my bag up to the third floor, which I share with a denture maker and a young defense attorney who works nights in the neighborhood.

The Trojan is an anachronism, a giant brick building with a full-size gymnasium and high-ceilinged pool area in a city where property is priced by the cubic inch, and most of the new health clubs are microexercise centers roosting on the top floors of hotels and residential skyscrapers. The spacious offices on the third floor of the Trojan were an afterthought of the builder and just a sideline for Barbi, the owner of the club. Half of them are vacant because Barbi rents only to people she likes, and she has eccentric tastes in people.

Barbi bought the Trojan twenty years ago, when it was a men's bathhouse. She closed down the old operation on one day's notice and reopened it as an after-hours refuge for dancers and other denizens of the Combat Zone, a place to go for a massage or a swim after a hard night on the streets. The clientele has gotten more upscale in the last few years, yuppies have discovered the place, but Barbi hasn't changed anything to accommodate them. I've been her tenant for seven years now, and I guess I'm something halfway between a denizen and a yuppie newcomer.

My office smelled stale and disused, so I opened the window on Charles Street and let in the sound of traffic. The theater across the way was playing two movies, the latest Rambo and *Friday the 13th, Part VII*—or maybe it was only one movie, and Rambo and Jason had merged like Time and Warner Brothers. My other window offered a more relaxing view—it's on an inside wall, wire-mesh looking down to the twenty-five-meter indoor swimming pool. Barbi keeps the pool lights low, and I sometimes do my best thinking while staring down at the swimmers making slow laps in the lit green water, or staring up at my own lit windows while I make the laps myself.

I'd given Della the week off—she was still in the top drawer of my desk, and I got her out and put her to work, replacing my special vacation tape. Della's the message on my answering machine, recorded years ago by an actress friend who later went out to California to become a daytime television star. When she made the recording she gave it a lot of energy, pretending to be Perry Mason's girl Friday, Della Street. She always impresses my clients—a few of them have been seriously disappointed to learn she's unattainable. I keep a master copy of the recording in a safe deposit box, along with my childhood collection of Indian head nickels and my great-grandfather's gold pocket watch.

I had an hour before Mary showed up, and I used it well. Edgar, the aging ex-boxer who works as the club's masseur, had left my mail outside the door, and I took care of that quickly. The only interesting item was a membership offer from the NRA that included a free camouflage Thermos. A camouflage Thermos is something I could really use, so I put that aside and junked everything else.

By five o'clock I was ready to start work. I'd skimmed a

week's worth of headlines from Edgar's stack of old *Herald*s in
his basement office, so I was up on all the scandals that had
entertained the city during my absence. I'd had a cup of coffee
with Edgar, done ten quick laps in the pool, changed into a light-
blue suit I keep in the closet with my other disguises, and sat
reading the Hemingway biography I'd stolen from Sam. I'd remembered that Mary Wyman was a Hemingway buff. At five
after five Edgar stuck his bald head into the office and said,
"There's a beat-up old dame on the street wants to see you. She
won't come in."

"That's because she's eccentric," I said, and followed him
downstairs.

I hadn't seen Mary Wyman in six years, and back then I
hadn't known her well. She'd lived with her sister, and the sister
was dying. Mary hired me to find their long-lost brother—so he
could say his good-byes or attend the funeral, depending on how
quick I was. The brother turned out to be dead and the best I
could come up with was a long-lost niece who lived in Boston.
When I found the niece my involvement in the case ended.

Mary hadn't changed much since then. She stood waiting at
the curb, wearing a plain black dress, with gray hair held back
in a tight bun. But she now had deep bruises around both eyes
and a red scab with stitches showing over the right eyebrow.
She looked at me with cynical appraisal. I must have looked
okay, because when she spoke it was to comment on her own
appearance.

"I'm a mess, aren't I? I look like I belong on a park bench.
But I've got money." And she reached into a big pocket of the
black dress and pulled out a stack of bills. A guy walking by did a
double take, then kept moving when he caught my eye. I took the
money. "This isn't necessary," I said. "I get paid by the day."

"Consider it an advance—five thousand dollars. Money's

not my problem, I've got plenty. Did Michael tell you anything?"

"Only that you'd been mugged, and I could have guessed that."

"Let's see what else your eyes are good for. Bring your car around, if you've got one. I'll show you."

She slid onto the slightly tattered vinyl seat of the Rambler without comment, buckled her seat belt, and told me to drive out Columbus Avenue. She sat straight in the seat, looking grim and determined until we got to our destination in the South End. It was one of those short side streets that dead-ends on the old Boston & Providence railroad line, which for more than a century formed an unnatural boundary between the posh Back Bay and the down-at-mouth South End. The railroad bed is now a long, narrow park, with a fence along one side that continues to divide the neighborhoods. You could look up Mary's street and see the big dome of the Christian Science Mother Church in the near distance, beyond the backs of the buildings on St. Botolphe.

We got out of the Rambler. About half of the red brick, four-story town houses running down each side of the short block had been gutted—there were piles of plaster and dusty birch lathing spilling from plastic shoots suspended over blue disposal units on the sidewalks. One building had been fully renovated, brick steam-cleaned, all-weather glass windows installed, and small bushes planted by the front stoop. It looked uninhabited. Bolted to its side was a sign reading EDEN'S GARDEN—LUXURY TOWN HOUSES FOR THE FORTUNATE FEW. An artist's rendering showed the whole block looking rehabilitated, with a few fortunate people strolling down brick sidewalks under young maples on what was obviously a cool summer night in a little corner of yuppie paradise.

Mary pointed to a scruffy building in the center of the block, one that would never fit into the artist's rendering. "That's mine," she said. "I own it." She gave me a look that suggested I better get her point quickly, or she'd find somebody else to do whatever job she had to offer.

A big aelanthus, a weed tree, grew straight up the front of Mary's building. Its elegant pointed leaves only half obscured the stained brick and rotting windowsills. Around its base a garden of weeds grew out of control, littered with old bottles and bits of paper—obviously not the garden for which the new development was named.

"Mary Wyman," I said. "You're willfully impeding the course of progress and depriving the fortunate few of their slice of paradise."

Mary didn't smile. She looked from me to the building then heaved a small sigh of satisfaction. "Isn't it pretty to think so," she said.

The house was different inside. It reminded me of a 3-D slide of a turn-of-the-century room I'd recently seen through an old viewer in an antique shop in Maine. Two ornate mahogany and velvet sofas extended from each side of a black marble fire-place. There were mahogany tables, Tiffany glass lamps, lace doilies crowded with china figures of boys on horseback and girls holding bouquets. The wallpaper had a pattern of raised velvet flowers. In the entranceway an old grandfather's clock sported a hand-painted two-master under full sail and two brass plates showing both hemispheres of the planet earth.

"This room is older than I am," Mary said. "Mother bought the house, furnished, from the estate of a woman who'd lived here since the block was built, in the 1870s. Mother never changed a thing, except to install electricity, and I've done less than that. She moved us here after Father died, wanted to be close to the Christian Science church. She and my sister were believers."

"It's a nice room."

"Sit down. Of course it's nice, it's more beautiful than anything our culture has managed to put together in the last ten decades. It's got order to it. The only part I contributed was the books." She pointed to a double mahogany bookshelf built into the corner.

"I went to Radcliffe, you know, and just before Mother died, in 'forty-seven, I traveled to Paris to write books. It was cheap to live in Paris then. But Jennie, my sister, was ill. She wouldn't see doctors, and with Mother gone, I had to come home to care for her. Damn fool thing to do. I sometimes think Mother died just to bring me back from Paris. I've been here ever since. What will you have to drink?"

"Coffee?"

"It's after five," she said. "I'll bring you whiskey." And she went off toward the back of the house.

I looked at the books in the corner. There were rare editions of memoirs written by people who'd been lucky enough to live in Paris during the twenties and thirties, along with biographies of the same people and their fiction. I spotted the biography I'd just been reading, which told me Mary was keeping current on all the latest Hemingway minutiae.

She came back with two highball glasses of straight whiskey, no ice.

"That's where I hide from life," she told me, nodding at the books.

I took one of the glasses and we sat on opposite sides of the coffee table by the fireplace. The whiskey was a single-malt Scotch. I'd once walked into the bar at the Bombay Hunt Club five minutes after a man I'd come to see had swallowed Scotch laced with cyanide, and I think of that whenever I drink the stuff. Mary finished half of hers and set down the glass.

I looked at the bruises around her eyes and said, "When did it happen?"

"Last Tuesday night. Late. I walk at night, it's a habit I developed when I was caring for my sister, Jennie, and needed to get away from this place. I'm never afraid—I know I look like a street person, Mr. Mallory, not worth robbing, and certainly not worth raping."

I didn't tell her there were people out there who wouldn't care how she looked. I said, "You think the attack had something to do with the real estate development going on outside?"

"Eden's Garden," she said with disgust. "If I were religious, I'd call that blasphemy. There's no doubt about the connection. I'd been threatened by those people. I ignored the threats, and this is what they did to me. I don't intend to ignore them any longer, I intend to fight back. That's why you're here."

"How were the threats made?"

"By telephone. I'd disconnect the damned thing, but Michael won't let me. A man called and said I should move, that I'd be sorry if I stayed. I hung up on him, figured he was just a nut. He called back right away and said something obscene, something he'd do to me if I didn't move out. It went on like that every night after, for a month."

"But you own this place. They couldn't get their hands on it just by forcing you to move out."

"Michael agrees with you, says it doesn't make sense. But that's what the man on the phone wanted. Ask him what it's all about, when you find him."

"What about other people living on the block?"

"They're mostly old people. My neighbor was beaten so badly he's still in the hospital. That was last Saturday night.

Those with telephones get calls, others get rocks through the windows. They're all tenants of something called Eden Development. Eden can't throw them out because they were here under rent control, so it's trying to drive them out. Michael says they've probably lumped me in with the rest somehow, or they figure I'll get tired of it and sell."

"So what has Michael done about Eden?"

"He can't find them. That's the problem. You'll have to talk with Michael about that. I only know it's a nightmare. I used to think things were bad for my neighbors when that skinflint Anthony D'Amato ran all those buildings. But the new breed of skinflints are from a whole other level of hell."

"When did Eden take over?"

"Just this last year, but before that D'Amato got too old and sick to handle things himself and hired a management company. All they cared about was money, money, money, but never any to fix a broken pipe or replace a pane of glass. A lot of the old tenants moved out. That's when I started letting the outside of my place go to pot—no reason to keep it up.

"Unfortunately, I'm tied to this house by years and by people long dead, Mr. Mallory. I'd never sell, especially not after what they've done to me. I'd die first." Tears started to run from her right eye, and she took a handkerchief from a pocket and dabbed at it angrily. "I'm not crying," she said. "When that animal hit me in the face he damaged a nerve, and this is what happens to me."

"Tell me about him."

"He wasn't big like you, maybe five nine, with skinny arms. Big enough to handle me, though. He wore a wool mask, like skiers do. From his hands I would say he was white, or maybe Hispanic."

"Why Hispanic?"

"He had an accent. It was midnight. He grabbed me by the

throat and hit me across the face three times, then let me drop. He
leaned over me, he smelled like death, and he said, 'Next time I
come with a knife.'" She reached for the glass of Scotch and
finished it.

"Was it the same person who'd made the threatening calls?"

"I think so. His voice was muffled over the phone, but he
had the same accent. He left me lying there, I'd fainted. About
three in the morning a neighbor found me and took me to the
hospital. Fred—he's a young man, a veteran, served in Vietnam,
and now he drives a taxi."

"What have the police done?"

"The police are morons, you ought to know that. Michael
reported the attack, but nothing came of it. They say it's random
violence. I've got a gun to protect myself, and Fred watches over
me when he can."

Everyone I met these days had a gun. I said, "You want me
to find who's behind Eden?"

"That's right. And stop them. I don't like being threatened
and manhandled, and I don't like greedy people who have to
take, take, take all the time. Everyone these days is taking, and
making money, and nobody's happy. If you're happy they come
after you." I caught the echo of a line from Hemingway: If
you're good, they kill you. Mary got up from the couch and went
to the bookcase, pulled out one of the books, and grabbed a stack
of bills from behind it. "This is ten thousand dollars. If you stop
them, it's yours."

"Does all your money come in bundles?"

"I like to have it around. Most of my inheritance is handled
by the Boston Company, Michael sees to that. It's Michael you
have to talk with now. I've told you everything I know."

There was pounding from the back of the house, and I raised
an eyebrow at Mary. "The doorbell doesn't work," she said.

I headed for the back, passing through a short hallway where a staircase led to the upper floors. There was a white Angora cat sitting on the stairs. Mary came behind me, after stashing the money back in the bookcase. I opened the kitchen door and stepped into a Booth cartoon.

I couldn't get an accurate count on the number of cats in the room, since they moved too quickly, but I figured fifteen at least. Three of them were brushing against my legs, the way they do when they think you don't like them. There were two kittens that came tumbling over to play with Mary's shoelaces.

More pounding at the back door, and through the glass I saw a woman in her forties, big-boned and mean-looking.

I turned to Mary.

"You must remember my niece, Caroline," she said. "Should we let her in?"

When I opened the door Caroline said, "Who are you and what are you doing here?"

Mary said, "Don't be a fool, Caroline. You know he's a private investigator. I told you I was going to hire him."

"Of course," Caroline said, shifting gears so suddenly the glare became an ingratiating smile in one quick twist of her lips. "I remember you now. I'm Caroline Peabody." She reached to shake hands. "What do you propose to do to protect my aunt?"

"I don't need protection," Mary said. She stooped to pick up the two kittens, one in each hand, and held them to her chest. "I just want to be left alone."

But that was obviously more than Caroline could manage. "Don't you think it would make sense for Aunt Mary to come stay at my home until this trouble is settled, Mr. Mallory? As you know, my husband and I live on Beacon Hill." She said it like the Hill was a church where people went for sanctuary.

"And what would I do with my cats?"

"Bring them along."

"Hogwash," Mary said.

"I don't want to be a person who tries to make decisions for her elders," Caroline said, then turned to me. "But don't you think she might be in danger, Mr. Mallory, staying here?"

My watch said it was six-fifteen. I took out a business card, the one with my home number as well as Della's, and handed it to Mary. She put the kittens down and took the card. "I'm meeting Michael at six-thirty," I said. "If you see or hear anything suspicious, call me. Try not to go out late at night, and keep the door locked."

"I have to go too," Caroline said. "Will you walk me to my car, Mr. Mallory?"

It had been a remarkably short visit, which didn't seem to displease Mary. She waved us both away and went toward the living room. Caroline raised her eyes to communicate her frustration with the situation. A cat got itself around her legs and she reached down for it, gave it a kiss on the top of its head, set it down on the counter beside the door, and went on out. It was a gesture of tenderness that surprised me. The cat gave me a smug look, and I followed Caroline, making sure the door locked behind me.

She waited on the porch, where there were more cats. A baby-blue Cadillac sedan was parked at the foot of the steps. Across the wide alley the buildings had already been fully gentrified—cedar decks at each floor, cluttered with bottled-gas barbecues and ten-speed bikes fixed to the railings with kryptonite locks.

"Well?" she said. "It's obvious, isn't it, that my aunt's insane?"

"Is it?"

She continued as if I had agreed with her. "I could have had her committed five years ago, but I've never wanted to be that kind of person. But it's tragic, she's a prisoner in that place. My father was strong enough to leave when he was young, and he never returned. Please see that she comes to stay with me?"

"I'll certainly do everything I can to help Mary," I said.

She smiled, said "Thank you," then got in the Cadillac in one quick motion, pushed a button that made all the locks go *clunk,* and drove out of the alley without another word. It was clear I'd done Mary no favor by finding her niece six years earlier, and clear also that if Mary loved peace and a sense of order, she'd never find it at Caroline's house. I was running late, so I headed for the Rambler. Driving into town, I wondered briefly if Caroline had any ulterior motives pushing her to take Mary in. Meanwhile, half my brain was still working on the problem of Hank Tuttle.

CHAPTER SIX

Property
Is Theft

I PARKED ILLEGALLY on Province Street and walked around the corner to the Parker House, where two uniformed attendants stood on the sidewalk waiting to open limousine doors. They wore tails and top hats, like Cinderella's magic footmen. I went in through the brass revolving doors and down a staircase lined with oak paneling and photos of nineteenth-century businessmen. The downstairs pub was dimly lit and crowded with well-dressed women and men who'd stopped for a quick one after work, then stayed on, getting louder, happier, and less intelligent with each new round.

I found Michael alone at a table for four. He spotted me coming and waved, and when I made it through the crowd to the table he said, "Long time no see, Jimmy. What you drinking?" He waved to a waitress carrying a tray of drinks. She ignored him.

Michael's in his early forties, almost completely bald, with a shiny round head and amiable expression like Charlie Brown's—which probably explains why waitresses, hotel clerks, and opposing counsel often make the mistake of thinking he's a wimp. He cultivates the image, like one of those tropical spiders that resembles a harmless yellow flower, until the fly's in the net and the spider moves in for the kill. That night Michael wore a light-gray summer suit from Brooks Brothers, brightened by one of the starched pink shirts he has shipped from an exclusive shop in London, a scarlet bow tie with matching handkerchief in the breast pocket, and green suspenders.

When I got seated Michael said, "Caroline crash your meeting with Mary?"

"She did. Thanks for the advance warning."

He chuckled. "Poor Caroline just wants to be loved. She's married to old Winfred Peabody, and Winfred doesn't love anything but the gold in his safe deposit box. Got a mansion on Beacon Hill where Mary'd be safe and well cared for. The only drawback would be Caroline and Winfred."

"Does Winfred own real estate in the South End?"

Michael smiled. "That's a point, for all I know even Winfred could be behind Eden Development. I suppose that might explain Caroline's desire to see Mary out of that house. But I doubt it."

"Tell me about Eden."

"They're an enigma, Jimmy. After Mary got hurt I finally got off my butt and took some action. Or tried to. We went into court, filed a complaint for a restraining order and damages. But we couldn't find Eden Development to serve process. It's like chasing a ghost."

"Who's we?"

"Me and Phil Levine—legal services lawyer representing the tenants on Mary's block. That's another thing. Whoever's behind Eden has somehow linked Mary to the tenants—it's like they didn't bother to give precise instructions, just 'go out and beat up anyone who lives on the block.'"

The waitress showed up and I ordered a Budweiser. Michael said, "Here's Levine now."

I turned and spotted a dark-haired guy coming across the room. He was at least six three and skinny, probably 160 pounds max, wearing jeans and a tweed jacket. From the neck down he looked like Ichabod Crane. Above the neck he had a warm, lazy smile and dark eyes that fixed on the waitress and held her in place until he'd gotten seated and ordered a double Jack Daniels on the rocks. On the lapel of his jacket a small green button said PROPERTY IS THEFT.

"Phil Levine, meet Jim Mallory."

"The detection maven," Levine said, and reached across to shake. I could feel all the long bones of his hand, but the grip was firm.

"I've just started to tell Jimmy about our anonymous friends at Eden Development."

"How can Eden own real estate, pay taxes, rent apartments, and manage to stay anonymous?" I said.

"Anything's possible when there's big money at stake," Levine told me, giving Michael a sideways glance. "Ask my co-counsel about that, he specializes in the kind of protection big money can buy." Michael just grinned at him, like it was a running joke between them.

"That neighborhood's like a vein of pure gold," Michael said. "Classic brick and brownstone buildings, a stone's throw from Back Bay."

"So Eden bought itself a high-priced attorney," Levine went on, "to set up the deal in a way that keeps us from getting to them."

"Who're the lawyers?"

"Bill Amory, from Amory and Harcourt," Michael told me.

I knew the firm. One of the partners had once tried to hire me to follow his wife, and got offended when I told him I didn't do divorces. Amory & Harcourt was a waspy Brahmin institution that had been around when the South End was nothing but a spit of brush-covered sand connecting Beacon Hill to the mainland. "I didn't think lawyers like that represented thugs," I said.

"Times are changing. I've known Bill Amory for years. He

told me Eden insisted on anonymity, that the firm's representation ended with the consummation of the purchase of the real estate last May, and he couldn't help me beyond that."

"He lied," Levine said.

"Maybe," Michael conceded. "The firm has had financial difficulties—if Eden looked like a good long-term client, they might have grabbed at the business with no questions asked."

"Did Eden just pick Amory out of the phone book?"

"Don't know. Someone called Bill's son, George, on a no-names basis. Then sent along a bag of cash to handle the fees. A paper sack, full of hundreds. Bill tells me he didn't know about that aspect of the deal until after the closing—the kid ran it through accounting without mentioning the method of payment. I got that much out of him in the locker room at the Bombay. Then he clammed up on me. Stopped answering my phone calls about a week ago."

"What was the purchase price for Eden's Garden?"

"Five million. A bargain."

"Wouldn't the lawyer who represented the other side have files of documentation on the buyer?"

"It's the financing bank that asks for a paper trail from the purchaser," Michael said. "For this deal, cash money got sent by wire transfer from two accounts in the Cayman Islands. Seller's lawyer told me that much."

"So the money's untraceable," I said. "But why two accounts?"

"The deeds show Eden as a general partnership. Could be two partners with separate accounts. Massachusetts general partnerships don't have to register, so we don't have the names of any principal, not even straw owners. D'Amato, the former owner, had hired a realty company to manage things, and they'd already laid down a master deed for the condos—so Eden didn't even have to make any filing with the state for that."

"So what went on between May and now?"

"Nothing changed—they kept the same management company, South End Realty, and didn't try to raise rents. Then the phone calls started, about a month ago. Phil knows more about that end of it."

"Threatening phone calls and then beatings," Levine said. "I deal with it all the time. Eden added a few new twists—like being invisible. Even the management company doesn't know how to contact them; they've been holding rents in an escrow account since May. Their only point of contact is a local post office box."

"Why not serve the management company with the complaint? They're Eden's agents."

"We tried that. They came into court at the hearing for the preliminary injunction and convinced the judge they weren't a proper party. She threw us out of court."

"Tell Jimmy what you told me about the pattern of this thing," Michael said.

Levine shrugged. "There are a lot of ways Eden Development differs from the ordinary tenant-busting landlord. The typical landlord resorts to violence in amateur ways—usually because he thinks the laws are set up to screw him, so he's always there in the background, citing his rights under the Constitution. And it's usually easy to connect him to the people beating on heads. Often they turn out to be his own building managers." He took a sip of the Jack Daniels. "Eden's people are unusually violent," he added. "A recalcitrant landlord most often starts by shutting off basic services, like heat and water. Eden Development went straight into violence. They don't seem to care about bad publicity or even the possibility of criminal prosecution. You know what my worst fear is—that their next step will be to start burning people out. They scare the hell out of me."

"We need to find out who we're dealing with," Michael said. "That's where you come in, Jimmy."

"And we need the information fast," Levine added. "Landlord-tenant battles are won by whichever party holds out longest. The longer it takes us to get an injunction, the more tenants we'll lose, and the less chance of getting the courts to back us."

"What do you know about Harvey Blackstone?" Michael said.

I raised my eyebrows. "Slum landlord, owns most of Roxbury and the South End. People say he got his start laundering mob money through real estate deals, but that was years ago. Still goes out to dinner with the kingpins from time to time, and the *Herald* likes to print photos whenever he does. Why?"

"We think it's possible Blackstone's the man behind Eden," Levine told me. "He was negotiating to buy out D'Amato when Eden showed up from out of nowhere and agreed to pay the asking price in cash. We think maybe that was just a change of strategy, that maybe Blackstone decided at the last minute he had some cash to bury and came up with the Eden scam."

"Someone else's cash?"

"Not necessarily. A lot of Blackstone's rents are paid in cash, so he may have been looking for his own unofficial tax shelter."

"If that was the case," Michael said, "you'd think he'd sit on the property, keep a low profile."

"Which is what Eden did at first," I said.

"So maybe there was some kind of power struggle within the partnership, if there was a real partnership, that caused the change of strategy? Makes sense, but I don't know where it gets us."

"A lot of maybes," I told him, "but that's better than nothing. That post office box for Eden—is it still active?"

"Far as I know. Private mailbox service, on Mass. Ave., down by the river. Your neighborhood." Michael gave me the street address and box number, 331.

Levine finished his drink and looked at his watch. "I've got to run off to a tenants' meeting. As you've probably guessed, my clients can't afford to pay for a private detective, Mr. Mallory, but Michael's letting us come along for the ride."

"In return for a lot of expertise in housing law from you," Michael said.

"A simple exchange of values, like chopping wood for your dinner. I'm just a hobo lawyer." He smiled as he stood up and reached to shake my hand. He said, "Good luck, Mr. Private Eye. I look forward to hearing your report."

We watched him thread his way through the crowd, turning a few heads. Michael said, "He's a hell of a good lawyer, could be pulling in three, four hundred grand a year at a private firm, and the state's probably paying him forty." He finished his beer and said, "What else can I tell you, Jimmy?"

"You think Eden wants Mary's house bad enough to kill her for it?"

"God knows. A woman her age could have been killed by that beating. All the more reason to get to Eden quickly, which I'll leave to your talents." He grinned. "This is crazy, but I'm taking my kid to a Grateful Dead concert tonight, and I'm already late. Can I give you a ride?"

"I'll walk out with you." Since he'd just given me a hint of what his annual income amounted to, I didn't protest when Michael picked up the tab. On our way out I spotted a familiar face at a table across the room. I told Michael to go ahead without me.

He said, "Call if you get anything at all," and headed up the stairs.

I went over to the table and said hello to Dana McOscar.

*   *   *

She was drinking St. Pauli Girls with three men. My arrival interrupted the man on her right, who was telling a story that didn't seem to interest the others. All three men looked too young to be wearing the expensive gray suits and silk ties that told me they were lawyers. The looks they turned in my direction suggested I was too old to be saying hello to Dana McOscar—but she gave me a surprised smile of recognition and said, "Mallory."

Seeing her again made me happy in a way I hadn't expected. She was still wearing the blue suit and Ralph Lauren blouse she'd had on that morning. But with her long blond hair and bright-blue eyes she looked as exotic and out of place at the table of gray men as she had strolling through the Sangerville woods.

"Jim Mallory, meet George, Frank, and Peter," she said. "Mallory's a private eye. Won't you join us?"

Frank got up to fetch another chair. George, the one I'd interrupted, leaned closer to Dana and shot me a nasty look. He wore suspenders, his hair was slicked back on both sides of a narrow head, and his pointed nose supported round, horn-rimmed glasses. The glasses made him look like a fashion model trying to look like a lawyer.

Peter said politely, "A private eye? That must be interesting."

"Mallory's working on the Judge's brother's murder," Dana answered for me.

I didn't contradict her. The same waitress came by to ask if I wanted another Budweiser. George said quickly, "We just want the check," but Dana ignored him.

"I'll have a beer," I said, then remembered I hadn't eaten since the cheeseburger I'd picked up at a Burger King on the

Maine Turnpike. I ordered two ham sandwiches. "I'm surprised to see you back in town," I said to Dana.

"Flew back this afternoon. I don't like funerals." She took a drink of her beer directly from the bottle, keeping her head deliberately turned away from George's side of the table. "The Judge told me something about you that really surprised me," she said. "That you were one of his students at Harvard Law School. That you dropped out after first year."

"I confess."

"How come?"

I wondered if she was tipsy or just trying to annoy George. The conversation was clearly having that effect, and she seemed aware of it.

"My father died," I said. "He'd wanted me to be a lawyer, but after he was gone it didn't seem so important."

George had shown a sudden, unexpected interest. "Was your father a lawyer?" he said.

"Social worker. But he'd always wanted to be a lawyer. I think he would have liked being a private eye even better."

George frowned and said, "We have dinner reservations, Dana." He stood up and stared at the waitress as she waited for the bartender to run the check through the register. Frank and Peter also got up, but Dana stayed seated, looking at me.

It got uncomfortable after a minute had passed and the waitress still hadn't brought the check. I said, "If you'll excuse me, I have to make a phone call." I stood up, said to Dana, "Maybe I'll see you when I drop by to talk with the Judge," gave a short wave to the others, and went off to the phone booth by the bathrooms. I called Della, but there were no messages from Mary or anyone else. I figured Dana and her boy lawyers would be gone by the time I got back to the table, but I was wrong. Dana was still there, alone, eating one of my sandwiches.

I sat down and she said, "Sorry for the scene with George."

"Was it a scene? It was a little confusing—is he your boy-friend?" She looked so young sitting there munching on the sandwich that the word boyfriend didn't seem inappropriate.

"It's a long story. I fell in love with George when I was One-L and he was third year. I thought he was wonderful then, and he helped me through a hard time in my personal life. Then he went to work at a large firm and got very serious and pompous. But you don't care about that, do you?"

She rattled it off like a story she'd told too many times to too many friends. I said, "It's interesting what happens to people when they become lawyers. It changes them in different ways."

"I wanted to talk with you about Ben," Dana said abruptly. "That's really why I stuck around."

"Talk away."

"Can we go somewhere else? I'm tired of this place."

I said "Sure," wrapped the sandwich I hadn't started in a paper napkin to stick in my pocket, left a tip, and we went together over to the cashier to settle my tab. When we stepped out onto School Street it was dark, and through the wrought-iron fence surrounding the old city hall we could see flickering candles lighting up wineglasses at the white linen tables of Maison Robert. "Still hungry?" I said.

"Maybe you could drive me home. I live in Monument Square. That's Charlestown."

"I know it well." We walked around the corner to the car. Dana didn't say anything at first as we drove through the maze of dark streets out to Congress. Then she suddenly became animated, and told me about how well she remembered all the little knobs on a '69 Rambler, which, she reminded me, had been her first car.

"I lost my virginity in that car," she said. I decided then she was definitely tipsy.

I said, "What kind of a name is McOscar, anyway?"

"Irish. Maybe that's why I decided to live in Charlestown."

Charlestown is indeed an Irish neighborhood. It's built on a long ridge of land rising from the harbor and running along what used to be the banks of the Mystic River. It's mostly frame houses and working-class triple deckers, except for a rehabilitated fringe of town houses around the old shipyard and the more elegant four-story brick buildings of Monument Square. A two-hundred-foot-high granite obelisk was built on a rise of ground in the center of the square, to commemorate the battle for Bunker Hill.

The obelisk is surrounded by green lawns and wrought-iron fences. I've sometimes walked out there on a good night in summer, just for the view of the skyline you get from its base. Dana's building was on the far side of the square. I stopped in front and she said, "Oh, shit."

"What?"

"See that Jaguar parked at the corner?"

"George's car?"

She nodded.

"He does well for himself."

"His father's senior partner at Amory and Harcourt. George was born well."

I thought it was an interesting coincidence that Dana's boyfriend was the man who'd once represented Eden Development, and that he'd crossed my path that night—but I couldn't see how it could be anything but coincidence.

"I was going to ask you up for coffee," Dana said, "but that wouldn't be a good idea now. I do have something to tell you. Maybe we could have dinner tomorrow night?"

"Are you sure what you have to say will keep?"

"It'll keep." She got out of the car. "Meet me at the courthouse, at six?"

"It's a date."

She smiled and closed the door. I watched her walk down the sidewalk to the Jaguar. I put the Rambler in gear, and as I passed the sleek little sports car, Dana got in the passenger's seat, beside George, and leaned across to kiss him.

I drove across town to Mary's, circled the block once, and parked in a shadowed part of the wide alley in back, a few houses down from hers. I'd had a long day, and I might fall asleep in the car, but at least I'd be close. I reached into the backseat for the Thermos I'd filled earlier that day, in Maine. There was still a quart of lukewarm coffee left. I rummaged in the glove compartment, found my pewter flask half full of Metaxa brandy, and poured some into the coffee to heat it up.

Certain kinds of liquor always stir certain memories—of course I'd known that when I filled the flask. Metaxa makes me think of sitting in a restaurant on the north coast of Crete, watching the big waves of a storm crash into the high breakwater of the harbor, sending sheets of spray over the fishing boats. If the storm hadn't lasted three days, I might have made it back to Ios in time to change the way a few things turned out. If that had happened, I might still be living there, instead of parked in an alley in the South End drinking lukewarm coffee.

Not that I minded. I loosened my tie, took out the sandwich from the Parker House, and settled back to enjoy my dinner.

CHAPTER SEVEN

After Midnight

I MUST HAVE DOZED OFF. I heard a light thump on the Rambler's front hood, opened my eyes, and saw a startled yellow cat crouched, staring at me through the windshield. My eyes went automatically to Mary's building and spotted a dark figure up on the back porch. There was a wrenching sound as the guy on the porch jimmied the lock with a pry bar, then a snap of splitting wood, the back door came open, and he froze, looking up and down the alley. A full minute went by before he went in.

I was out of the car and running down the alley by the time the door closed. I glimpsed a flashlight beam inside the kitchen, slowed, and went up the steps cautiously, peered through the glass of the old door. The prowler wore a black ski mask, had set the flashlight on the counter, and was rummaging in a drawer beside the stove. He came up with a long, silver carving knife that flashed in the random light through the kitchen windows. He held it daggerlike, left-handed, taking practice swipes. He seemed to enjoy the feel of it. Then he made stabbing motions with the pry bar in his right hand, as if trying to decide if that felt as good. I started to ease open the door, but as soon as it showed a crack one of Mary's cats scrambled through and the thug turned and spotted me.

He hurled the pry bar. The blunt end hit my left shoulder, numbing the arm, then bounced onto the counter. I snatched it up with my right hand and swung it in an arc as he came at me. He backpedaled out of range and I followed, grappling, dropping the pry bar to grab the hand with the knife. Mary had said her assailant smelled like death—at close quarters this one gave off a strong stench of rancid sweat. The cats were in a panic to get out of the room. We tripped over a mass of scrambling fur and claws and went down, both grunting.

When he hit the ground the carving knife skittered away, but my left arm was still numb from the shoulder down and I couldn't hold him. Like the cats, he seemed to be in a big hurry to get out of that room, scrambling away toward the hallway leading to the front of the house. I was five steps behind, but when I'd navigated through the antique living room and reached the front stoop he was already on the sidewalk and running, heading toward the park. I kept after him.

A car appeared from nowhere and raced along parallel to me, a flash of white matching my speed. Just before I cleared the last of the dumpsters that lined the sidewalk, the car accelerated, shot forward, and swung up over the curb to block my path.

I put both hands out and vaulted over the front hood, but my left ankle didn't clear the far fender and I went down on the cement sidewalk, managing a shoulder roll that kept me from breaking bones. The driver's door flung open and a bald white guy with a Fu Manchu mustache popped out, glanced at the vanishing thug, then swung a big handgun at my head. "Freeze!" he yelled, a sharp edge of panic in his voice.

I stayed on the ground, listening to the running steps disappear up the street. The white Chevy had CITY LINE TAXI stenciled in red letters on the side.

I tried to get my breath to say something but all that came out was "Fred." It had to be the vigilante neighbor who'd found Mary and taken her to the hospital a week earlier.

Mary's head and shoulders appeared over the hood of the

taxi. She was wearing a robe and nightgown, and her long gray hair hung over her shoulders. She squinted at me and said, "It's Mallory, Fred. Don't shoot him."

When the cruiser showed up Mary was in the kitchen, sulking. She didn't like cops and was disappointed in me because I'd insisted on calling them. I sat on a couch in the parlor sipping Scotch from a highball glass. When the knock came I got up to let them in—two uniformed patrolmen, one gray-haired and too old to be working the graveyard shift, the other a young black man. The latter directed his eyes at a broken lamp the thug had overturned on his way out, then at Fred who sat in a chair against one wall, then back at me. The old guy directed a hungry look at my glass of Scotch.

"You reported a breaking and entering," the young cop said.

I explained the situation and gave him my ID. He said, "Let's get your statement." To his partner he said, "Maybe you better check out that taxi off the curb, Harry."

"It's mine," Fred said, but Harry went out anyway, and didn't come back.

I told the story. When the young cop had it all down in his notebook he wanted to talk with Mary, and I went out to the kitchen for her. She'd dressed and put her hair up in a bun, and now she was drinking Scotch—she finished the two fingers left in the bottom of the glass in one swallow, then followed me back out to the parlor.

It was almost dawn before the cop finished getting everything down. He put the abandoned knife in a plastic bag for fingerprinting—even though I'd told him the perpetrator had worn gloves—and said city detectives would be in touch. I knew that wasn't likely since nobody had been hurt and nothing had been taken from the house, but at least there'd be a record of the break-in if Michael needed it next time he went to court.

The cop told Fred to move his taxi off the sidewalk, and went. Fred followed. I closed the door and turned to Mary. "We've got to move you out of here."

"No," she said.

I was tired. I said, "Somebody came here tonight, maybe to kill you. I don't intend to spend my nights sleeping in your alley, or even on your couch. You stay here and I quit."

"I won't go to Caroline's. I don't like her, and I don't like her husband."

"That's fine. I have a friend who would probably have you as a guest, if you're willing. Her name's Barbi. She owns the Trojan Gym and Health Club, which you refused to go into this afternoon. She lives in Weston. If you went there we would tell nobody where you were—not Caroline, not even Michael."

"I haven't spent a night away from this house in forty years."

"It's about time, then."

"What about my cats?"

"I'll find someone reliable to feed them. It's the best we can manage, Mary. It won't be for long—a week at most."

"I'll go," she decided, adding with mild sarcasm, "I wouldn't want my death on your conscience. But I have to feed the cats first."

She headed for the kitchen while I got the phone and dialed. I knew Barbi well enough to understand that an emergency phone call at four-thirty in the morning was something she could handle. When she answered on the third ring I said, "It's Mallory."

There was no indication from her voice that she'd been sleeping. She said, "What's up?"

I told her about Mary, and she said, "Bring her out," and hung up.

Mary came into the room with a medium-sized suitcase. She wouldn't let me carry it for her. She hadn't gone to the book-case to check her nest egg, and I guessed she'd moved it after showing it to me that afternoon, and the money was now in the suitcase.

We went out the back door to the Rambler. The alley was still in shadow, but the tops of the buildings on Mary's side were lit with the first sunlight. The air smelled fresh and clean—it made me wish for a cup of coffee. I spotted Fred's taxi parked behind an apartment building several doors down.

We took the Mass. Turnpike west to Route 128 and then the exit for Weston. Mary didn't say much on the drive through Cambridge and Newton, except to comment on the ugliness of the commercial developments beside the highway—things had changed a lot since her last trip out of Boston. But once we got off the freeway and into the real suburbs, the country stopped being ugly and started looking like a million bucks. We traveled narrow, well-paved roads that meandered past homes tucked into forests of hardwoods on lawns that glistened with dew. Every driveway was equipped with a luxury four-wheel-drive vehicle and a black Mercedes.

Mary said, "I like this time of morning. Sometimes at dawn I walk to the park to see the ducks. They sleep on that island in the pond where they're safe. I sit under the bridge and listen to them."

"Sounds nice."

"You should tell me it's not safe. That's what Caroline says, but who's going to hurt a shabby old lady?"

A thug with a penchant for knives and a bad case of body odor, I thought, but didn't say anything.

"You know what I think about by the pond," she said, "in the early morning?"

"What?"

"Paris. I had a good year there before Mother died. I hung out with a wild bunch—I even met Hemingway. At dawn sometimes we'd ride taxis to Les Halles for onion soup, after a night of parties."

"They tore down Les Halles," I said, "and put up a shopping mall."

"They would. Do you like Hemingway?"

"His books? Sure."

"What I like about his writing is the sense of control. That the good things in life can be captured and preserved. You've never married?"

"No."

"Why not?"

"I never wanted to make the commitment."

"You didn't want to lose control," she said. "That's what happened when I made the commitment to care for my sister. I lost control of my life. That's why I dislike needy people. Like Caroline. Are you happy, Mallory? That's a silly question. I haven't been happy for years, that's the only reason I ask."

I didn't say anything.

"Aren't you going to tell me it's never too late to be happy?"

"No."

"I'm getting old," she said.

We were driving up a hill through suburban woods. I turned off onto a dirt driveway that ran a hundred yards through trees, then opened onto lawns and gardens running up to a glass and stone house on the crest of the hill. Barbi was standing at the rail of the wide wooden deck, wearing a blue leotard with white shorts. She was slim and beautiful, with short-cropped brown hair and an ageless athlete's body.

I don't know where Barbi got the money for a house in Weston. She doesn't talk much about her past, but once in a while she lets slip a hint that suggests it was a wild one. She's an expert in methods of self-defense and may have once been a CIA agent. I knew that when the Rambler crossed a certain point in the driveway, an alarm had sounded inside the house, and that's why Barbi was waiting for us on the deck.

Mary tried to get out of the car, but she didn't look as if she'd make it, so I got around to her side to help. It was the first time I'd seen her behave like an old woman. Barbi came down the steps and together we got her into the house and onto a guest room bed. She mumbled something about needy people. We left her and went out to the porch.

"She's not an invalid," I said to Barbi. "She's had a rough night."

"Can you tell me about it?"

I did, in detail, and she listened in her characteristic way, head slightly cocked to one side.

"I could ask around, see if anyone knows anything about Eden," she suggested.

"Do it with a light touch. The important thing is to keep Mary incommunicado until I've got this worked out."

She smiled and put her hand in mine. "You look beat, Jimmy. Want some coffee?"

"I'd love some, but I'd better get back to town."

I left her standing on the deck, got in the Rambler, and headed back to Boston. I felt light-headed from lack of sleep, but relieved to know Mary would be safe with Barbi—at least as safe as anyone could ever be.

CHAPTER EIGHT

The Gates
of Eden

I SLEPT FOR FIVE HOURS, then left my apartment on Marlborough Street and walked around the corner to Security Plus, the private mailbox service that was our only known address for Eden Development. I hoped the service might have in its records some scrap of information about Eden that would help in my search for them—I'd either bribe it out of the proprietor or drop in later, after hours, to look for it myself.

Security Plus was a hole-in-the-wall enterprise two blocks up Mass. Ave. from Marlborough Street. Inside it was honeycombed with numbered post office boxes. At the end of the room the proprietor stood behind a window counter, talking on the telephone. On the wall over his head he'd tacked up hundreds of postcards, probably sent to former box holders and left unclaimed. As I waited for him to get off the phone I looked at the cards. There seemed to be one from every country in the world, including places Americans aren't supposed to visit, like Cuba and Libya.

The proprietor hung up, put the phone to one side under the counter, and turned to examine me. I wanted him to have that look of bribability—a cocky slant of the eye that suggests greed, cunning, and corruptibility all in one glance. Instead he looked intelligent and mildly interested in whatever I might have to say to him. He had a thin beard and mustache trimmed like Errol Flynn's but set in a round, amiable face. He said, "How can I help you?"

I posed as a new customer interested, for security reasons, in his methods of keeping records. He answered my questions without hesitation—as if any ulterior motive I might have would be irrelevant. The key to his security was a little MacIntosh computer behind the counter. The software was designed to thwart any nonfriendly attempt to access the confidential information. He kept no printouts or other hard copy on the premises. He didn't require my name or any personal data, but would take a forwarding address, along with a deposit to cover reposting the letters—in case I wanted the benefit of privacy without having to come back into the shop for my mail. The cost of a box was eighteen dollars per month, and I could pay as much as I wanted in advance—minimum two months rental.

I made one rather bare-faced attempt at a bribe, while he had his back turned, tapping me into the computer. "Bet you could tell some stories about the people who rent boxes," I said.

"It's an exciting business," he said over his shoulder, his voice expressing only mild sarcasm.

"You'd probably want to be reimbursed for the information," I added.

He turned and grinned. "What I sell here is privacy. It wouldn't make sense to expand my business beyond that. You still want a box?"

"Don't take offense," I said. "I'm just a careful man, checking all bases."

He smiled, didn't say anything, but took my two twenties off the counter. As the computer printed a receipt, he got four one-dollar bills from a brightly colored cigar box, wrote out the number of my new post office box on a slip of paper with a ballpoint pen labeled PROPERTY OF THE U.S. GOVERNMENT, and handed me a key. It was an interesting amalgamation of high-tech accounting and lemonade-stand economics. I left Security Plus,

caught the subway at Auditorium, and rode it downtown to Boyl-
ston and the Trojan Gym and Health Club.

I decided to call my friend Simon Mangenello, of the state
police detective bureau, and ask him to check through his files on
organized crime for any information about Blackstone that might
be helpful. He answered on the first ring, and I spent ten minutes
filling him in on Eden Development and the trouble at Eden's
Garden.

"If you want information about Blackstone, try back issues
of the *Phoenix*," he told me. "Once a year they do an exposé of
his exploitation of tenants in Roxbury and the South End."

"I'm more interested in the Mafia angle," I said. "Whether
he's still working scams for them—also, whether the situation at
Eden's Garden follows any pattern you've run into before."

"I'll look through my files. Far as I know, Blackstone got
out from under the yoke years ago."

"Check it out for me?"

"Sure. I'll use my imagination. In the meantime, I'll talk
with somebody on the Boston P.D. about beefing up patrols on
your old lady's block. Too bad you missed that guy last night—
you might have had your answer right there."

"Maybe I'll get another shot at him. Thanks for your help,
Simon."

My next stop was South End Realty. I took a dozen business
cards from my desk, the ones that say I'm James Maxfield of
Morgan Investments, a New York firm, and caught a cab to the
South End.

In that block of Columbus there were rows of spanking new
town houses on one side of the street—each with all the charm of

an architect's model displayed on a conference room table—and on the other burned-out storefronts and firetrap tenements waiting for rehabilitation. South End Realty was on the wrong side of the street. Not the type of place a man like James Maxfield would normally consult, but that might make its proprietors all the more eager to talk with me.

There was only one agent on the premises, a slim woman with huge glasses that hung down over her nose, focusing patches of light on her cheeks. I walked in and handed her my card without any comment. She slanted her eyes up at me, and bingo, there was the glance of greed, cunning, and corruptibility.

"How can I help you, Mr. Maxfield? I'm Irene Finch."

"I'll get right to the point," I said, sitting down. "I represent a consortium interested in a partially developed city block— Eden's Garden—owned by a partnership known as Eden Development. We have had no luck approaching Eden directly. Our local representative tells me you might help."

"You want to buy the property?"

"For six million, cash."

"Six million dollars?" she said, and I could see her doing the mathematics in her head—six percent times six million . . . the bottom line must have exceeded her capacity for fantasy, because she frowned and said resignedly, "I don't think they want to sell."

"I'll handle the negotiation with Eden. I want you to put me in contact with somebody authorized to represent them. For that, with adequate assurances of their authority, I'm willing to pay you a sixty-thousand-dollar finder's fee, in cash." I fixed her with a very businesslike look. "I emphasize the word cash for reasons that should be obvious. It would be a miscellaneous expense on our books, with no reference to the recipient."

"Let me make a phone call," she said.

She wanted to make it private, excused herself, and headed

for a back room. When she picked up the extension back there, a light came on at the phone on her desk. I lifted the receiver carefully. A woman's voice said, "Amory and Harcourt."

Irene got through to George Amory's secretary, but he was in conference. "Tell him to call Irene Finch," she said. "It's about Eden Development. Someone wants to buy in."

When she got back I was sitting in my chair, glancing impatiently at my watch. "Bear with me a few minutes," she said. "They'll call back."

The phone rang within ten minutes, Irene snagged the receiver, but it wasn't good news. As she listened, her smile slowly diminished. The voice on the other line was loud enough so I could hear it buzzing, though I couldn't make out the words. She hung up, looking displeased. "My contact is unavailable at the present time," she said.

I had the feeling George Amory hadn't been pleased to receive the call. I wanted to get as much information as possible before she went completely sour on me.

"What's the tenant situation at Eden? Has it been a problem?"

"Tenants are always a problem," she said distractedly. "That's why we like to convert to condos."

"Have you been helping the situation along–making life a little unpleasant for them?" I used a conspiratorial tone that implied my approval of such procedures, but she suddenly turned a hard look in my direction.

She picked up the business card and examined it, as if she could tell by the paper whether it was a phony. "Why don't I call you tomorrow?" she said. "Do you have a local telephone number?"

I said I'd call her. I tried one more shot. "Perhaps we should take our offer directly to Mr. Blackstone?" She didn't respond. I left.

*   *   *

I walked back toward my apartment and thought about Irene Finch. I could assume she hadn't called George Amory for legal advice—Michael had told me the management company was represented by a hack in the North End. That left two possibilities. Either George was still deeply involved with Eden Development, or Irene had simply remembered his name and hoped he might set up a meeting with Eden. But she hadn't left a number or company name with George's secretary. And the impression I'd had of the phone call back was of a subordinate being chastised by a superior.

I turned up Mass. Ave. and walked past the Christian Science Mother Church and then the Berkelee School of Music. I passed Security Plus—the proprietor was out front, locking the door for the night. Diagonally across the street, on my side, two men in gray business suits sat in a standard-issue black sedan. The man in the driver's seat was watching the proprietor through a pair of binoculars. I leaned close to the open window on the passenger's side and said, "Looking for someone?"

The man behind the wheel lowered the glasses and turned a pair of very cold eyes to examine me. The other one turned also. He said, "Move along." It was cop language.

"I'm a licensed private investigator," I said. "I may have an interest in whomever you're watching for, if they're related to Eden Development. Maybe we can talk."

No reaction, except "If you want to keep your license, friend, move along."

I moved along, noting the license plate number. I was pretty sure the black sedan hadn't been there earlier in the day. I added them to my list of things to have Simon check out.

CHAPTER NINE

Felicia's

AT A QUARTER TO SIX I left the Rambler in the lot behind the Trojan and walked across the Common, over Beacon Hill to Pemberton Square and the courthouse. A century and a half ago, Pemberton Square was a posh residential address, but the respectable brick town houses were torn down long ago and replaced by granite block government buildings—among them the Suffolk County Courthouse. The courthouse looks more like a high-security prison than a center of justice, with stingy little squares for windows and a narrow front entrance defended by cops and metal detectors.

At six in the evening there was only a single security guard chatting with Dana. I watched her turn and smile as I went through the revolving door. She looked young and lighthearted, wearing a light-blue summer dress and sandals. She seemed glad to see me, said good night to the guard, and took my arm. He gave me a quick smile of congratulation, then went back to reading his copy of *The Corpse Had a Familiar Face.*

Out in the square Dana said, "I'm starved."

"Feel like Italian?"

"Of course." So we negotiated the steps down to Court Street and started across the big empty plaza at Government Center. The harbor was out ahead of us, the sky over the harbor blue and hazy.

"Sorry for being a little drunk last night," she said. "I had a whiskey at the airport in Bangor with McGuire, then a whiskey on the plane, and when I showed up at court people were going out for drinks."

"I thought you were fine," I said. "How'd it go with George?"

"We had a fight. Then he wanted to come up and spend the night with me."

I didn't ask whether she'd let him. I said, "Breaking up is hard to do."

"You're being sarcastic, right? You saw George at his worst last night. He'd come from a hard day at work, a big deal he and his father are putting together. When George is under his father's thumb, he gets anxious. Then he tries to prove himself."

"Does he always work with his father?"

"Usually. Bill Amory's a workaholic. He puts a lot of pressure on George to be the same way. You'd think he'd have learned from past mistakes—his oldest son went to pieces under the weight of all those expectations. Died of a drug overdose. If anything, that just doubled the pressure on George. He sits in his office next door to Bill's, and he's within shouting range. Bill's a shouter."

"What does Bill think of you?"

"He thinks I'm cute."

I felt a little guilty using Dana to dredge up information about her boyfriend. But I wanted to have a good sense of what the Amorys were all about, before I approached them. I said, "George didn't have to go to work for his father."

"No. I suppose it was too much to expect of him, though, to resist being Amory the Younger at Amory and Harcourt. When I first met him he wanted to work for legal services, to make amends for some of the harm he felt his father had caused."

"I suppose everybody says that kind of thing when they start law school."

"True. I was going to be an environmental lawyer. Now I'm going to work for a big firm in Philly. But you broke from that pattern, didn't you?" she added, looking up at me. "Maybe that's why I like you."

"You're just tired of lawyers."

She laughed. "That's certainly true. In George's case, threatening to work for Legal Aid was probably just a way to punish his father. Like the son of a general who becomes a conscientious objector."

"When did you decide to go to Philly?"

"Always planned to. My parents are there." She looked up at me again and said thoughtfully, "I get your point though. I suppose if I'd taken George seriously, I'd have looked for work in Boston." She didn't say anything for a little while, and I didn't ask her any more questions about George for about a hundred yards. We went down more steps toward the waterfront and the Italian North End.

"Does George talk with you about his work?" I asked.

"Not really. I suppose that's my fault. I don't find it very interesting. It's all big corporations and banks, and I don't care about their problems."

I wondered how she was going to make out at the big firm in Philly. I said, "He represents Eden Development, doesn't he?"

"I don't know—I've never heard of them. Why?"

"Just curious."

She frowned but didn't say anything. We made our way past the block of old buildings that includes the Union Oyster House, then the pushcart vendors selling fish and vegetables in the shadow of an exit ramp off the expressway, to the tunnel that runs under the ramp and leads to the North End.

The North End is one of the oldest neighborhoods in the city—Paul Revere's house is there and the Old North Church where the signal lanterns got hung more than two hundred years ago. The Italian population arrived about a century after that, and much of the neighborhood now looks more Neapolitan than colonial. The meat vendors hang dead rabbits in their windows, the bakeries sell thick loaves of white bread, and cafés on Hanover Street fill the night air with the smell of strong coffee.

Felicia's is on the second floor of a building on a side street off Hanover. The walls of the staircase leading up to the dining room are crowded with photographs of celebrities posing with the owner, a short, red-haired woman in her sixties who looks a little like Margaret Thatcher. Since you always have to wait for a table, and the line forms on the staircase, there's plenty of opportunity to study the collection. Some of the photos are black and white and so old you can't identify the celebrity. I noticed two additions since my last visit—Ronald Reagan looking like a flushed Tweedle Dum and Rodney Dangerfield with a startled, disbelieving expression, as if Felicia had just goosed him.

There wasn't much of a crowd that night, and in fifteen minutes we'd been seated by the maître d' in a booth close to the staircase. The dining room is always dimly lit, with candles at the tables, the windows onto Richmond Street hung with heavy drapes. The decorations are eclectic but comfortable, knick-knacks and red velvet. The big waiters stand in a corner by the kitchen, stiff and formal in black tuxedos, each one looking like he could break your arm in ten places if you got out of line.

After we'd ordered Dana smiled and said, "What have you been up to since you got back from Maine?"

"Working on a new case. Real estate tycoons bashing tenants who are fighting back."

"Everything in this town boils down to real estate, doesn't it," she said, and then, "Do you always work for the little guy?"

"It's not that romantic. In this case I'm working for an eccentric woman with a trust fund."

"Is that why you asked me about Eden Development? It's a

funny name for a real estate firm. Developing the Garden of Eden. Almost like somebody's joke."

"Maybe that's what it is."

The waiter showed up with the wine, and I had to go through the ritual of tasting before he'd let us drink any. Dana said, "Is your work dangerous?"

"Last night somebody attacked me with a knife, and somebody else tried to run me down with a taxi."

"Right. Want me to ask George about Eden Development?"

"It's not important. Tell me why you invited me to dinner."

"That's easy. I want to hire you. To go back up to Maine, to help Hank Tuttle."

"Why?"

"You mean, why do I care? Do you have to know that?"

We stopped talking again when the waiter came back with our food. Along with the entrées came bowls of spaghetti with tomato sauce and a basket of hot bread. We made the appropriate noises of appreciation, and he left us alone.

"I'd want to know before I took the case," I said.

"It's a long story. Did you know Hank's dad was murdered? Twenty-five years ago."

"Shot by Hank's mother."

"That's right. They found her with the gun and the body, and she never spoke a word after that. She was dead within twenty-four hours. Killed herself."

"Did Hank tell you about that when you were a kid, helping with the cows?"

"He told me a few months ago. I know I told you I hadn't been in Sangerville recently, but that's because I didn't feel like explaining."

"Explaining what?"

"That I'm Hank's sister."

I stopped in midbite and looked at her.

"It's true. I was only a one-year-old at the time of the murder. Ben took Hank in, but the Judge arranged for me to be adopted. He was practicing in Dover-Foxcroft at the time, and he was friends with my adoptive parents. They'd been trying to have a child for years. They told me I'd been adopted as soon as I started law school—I guess, for them, that's when I became a grown-up. And that's when George was so nice, he understood, because his own mom died when he was only nine. You see, all of a sudden I felt like I'd lost both my parents."

"Does Hank know you're his sister?"

"I never told him. It's funny, he always used to tell me I looked like his mom. But the Judge says nobody in town knew who adopted me. The McOscars spent the next two summers in England—my father was writing a book. When they reappeared in Sangerville, they had a little girl, but there was no reason for anybody to make the connection."

"So you went up to Maine to find out about your parents?"

"Sure. And that's when Hank told me about how they died. Only he believes his father was murdered, not by his mother, but by somebody else in town."

"Somebody like Ben Chapman?"

"I don't know. I hope not."

"What else did he tell you?"

"He remembers the day of the murder clearly. He was out in the woods when it happened. My father worked in the mill in Guilford and had come home sick at lunchtime. One of the neighbors heard the shots and found my mother standing over the body, holding the gun. Hank got home after the police took her away. I was there with the neighbor. Hank took me out of the crib and ran for the woods. He was going to raise me out there, never come back. When I got hungry, he took me back to the neighbor's. By then our mother was already dead."

"And now he's run for the woods again."

She didn't seem to hear me. She said, "I was there while it all happened. My crib was right in the bedroom. Of course, I don't remember a thing. Anyway, Hank's my brother, and he needs my help."

"I have my eccentric client to take care of," I said. "Afterward, I'd planned to go up to Maine, to help Jay."

"When you do, I want to come with you, to be your client. I have money. In another month I'll be in Philadelphia, making a huge salary."

"Okay," I said.

She hadn't touched her food, but now she settled down to eat. I filled her glass and she drank half of it. "I could help you with the case you're working on," she said with a bright smile. "That way you'd finish quicker. My clerkship ends August thirty-first, but I don't have to start in Philly till October, so that gives us a little leeway."

"We'll see," I said. I sat drinking my wine while Dana finished eating. I looked for a family resemblance between her and Hank, but didn't find any, except the fact that she was tall. I started to wonder what she would have been like if she hadn't been given new parents as a one-year-old. She could be living on a farm now, the daughter of a millworker, probably married with five kids. As poor as Hank. And happy or not happy, depending on luck.

She paid for our dinner with an American Express card, and after it got whisked away she said, "I'd planned to take that card and make a run at Europe before I started work this fall. But I think it's important for me to go up to Maine."

"I'll make a deal with you. If we go up there, and you change your mind and decide to try Paris instead, don't be afraid to tell me." I hadn't meant it to be flirtatious, but I saw the ambiguity immediately—that I could be inviting myself along on her trip. She gave me a long, slow, speculative look.

The waiter came, Dana signed the imprint, and we squeezed through the latest batch of customers on the stairs and got back to Richmond Street. The sun was just starting to set, and I offered to walk her back to Charlestown. We followed Salem Street up the hill, and by the corner of Charter Street passed a group of people who'd brought kitchen chairs out onto the sidewalk for the relative cool. They were talking quietly in Italian, and everyone smiled at us. I think we made a handsome couple.

The Charlestown Bridge crosses the harbor at the mouth of the Charles River. It's covered with metal grating, the kind that hums when cars drive over it. Dana took my arm. I could see red navigation lights on the bridge pilings and to the right the outline of the USS *Constitution,* wooden masts strung with white lights. Beyond the marina was the obelisk on the hill, and to the far right a string of headlights coming off the Mystic Tobin Bridge.

When we got to Dana's door she said, "Come up for brandy? There's no George tonight."

"Raincheck?"

She nodded, stepped forward, and kissed me lightly. "Nobody wants a girl on the rebound," she said, then turned and walked up the steps. I hesitated a moment, then turned too and headed back into the city.

CHAPTER TEN

Security Plus

AN HOUR LATER I stood inside the front entrance of the private post office, having spent fifteen of the previous twenty-five minutes checking the neighborhood to make sure the black sedan wasn't still lurking nearby, five minutes picking the lock at the back door—only to discover it was bolted on the inside—and five more minutes waiting for an old man and his dog to make their slow way along the block and out of sight down Commonwealth Avenue so I could try the front. Security Plus didn't have an alarm system, which struck me as an anomaly—but the proprietor was probably so confident of his software security he didn't worry about the physical sanctity of the place.

Once inside I pulled the shade over the glass of the door. Light still poured in through the transom overhead, illuminating the collection of post cards on the opposite wall. I went directly to the MacIntosh behind the counter, turned on the power, and inserted diskettes. Then I sat in the green glow of the screen, listening. Somebody walked by on the street, and I held my breath until he'd passed.

The machine was asking for the password. I had to start somewhere so kept it simple, typed in SECURITY PLUS. The screen went blank, then a group of little monsters came out carrying letters that they assembled into two words, FUCK YOU. Not a very user-friendly response.

I always get a little nervous when I'm committing a crime

with maximum penalties in excess of five years. I started to wonder if I'd tripped a silent alarm after all, and if cops were even now racing across town to set up an ambush on the sidewalk outside.

I frowned at the screen. Maybe I'd have to resort to plan B—searching the proprietor's home during the day. He had to keep a printout of data somewhere, as a backup. But the fact that he'd programmed such an elaborate response to my incorrect guess on the password told me something about him. He liked a good joke. He was challenging me to find the punchline. That meant the answer wouldn't be completely random—such as the last four digits of his mom's telephone number—because then the game wouldn't be fair. At least, I hoped that's what it meant.

The screen was still asking me to give it a password, and underneath was the message, FUCK YOU. I typed in UP YOURS, and the little monsters came out and assembled FUCK YOU again, in larger, block letters. I tried another expletive and got the same response—this time the characters filled the screen and spilled over the edges. I finally got it. It was like the cookie monster virus that gets into your software and asks for a cookie; it freezes your screen until you type in COOKIE. I typed in FUCK YOU, and the thing scrolled out a page of data.

I'd been lucky—I was inside the program. In less than a minute I'd found the listing for box 331. It had been opened in late April, a year's rental paid in advance. The mail was to be held in the box for a week, then forwarded to another post office box, in Miami. Thanks to the media hype on the subject, my word association for MIAMI popped up DRUGS.

I copied out the address, replaced the diskettes, and turned off the machine. I found a master key hanging from a nail behind the counter and tried box 331. It was empty. A second key was labeled "front door"—I took that one with me, went back out to the sidewalk, locking the door behind me. There were no cops waiting. I had a copy of the key made at an all-night pharmacy, risked a second stop at the post office to return the original, then walked home to my apartment.

I live in a fourth-floor walkup on the last block of Marlborough Street, in the only building in Back Bay that hasn't been converted into condominiums. My landlord disappeared three years ago, and nothing can be done with the building until they find his body, or until the statutory seven years has run. I'm hoping he'll show up at the last minute with a good suntan, a lot of wild stories, and an irrational aversion to capital gains.

I didn't turn on the lights in the living room, but went through to the bedroom and sat on the bed to think about what I'd accomplished after a long day of turning over stones. I knew a little more about George Amory, and from Irene Finch's phone call, I had reason to suspect he was still involved in Eden Development's business. I knew that Eden had ties to Miami, and that its creators had been remarkably diligent in covering their footprints. I wondered if they'd gone to all that trouble just to frustrate efforts to serve them with process, or if there was a deeper reason. Tomorrow I'd take on a couple of bigger fish— George Amory and Harvey Blackstone. Michael had already tried asking straight questions. I'd try confrontation and see how they reacted.

Before going to bed, I filled an extra-large highball glass with ice and made a very strong whiskey and ginger ale, using the Old Bushmills I'd bought in Ireland. I went to the desk by the window and looked at the picture of Susan Johnson in the blue porcelain frame. I wondered if she was still in Greece.

It was almost midnight when I called Barbi. She sounded as fresh as she had that morning at five. I said, "How's Mary?"

"Well as can be expected. She's a tough old lady, Jimmy.

She was up for breakfast, then had some kind of reaction and slept till five. We had an early dinner, and we sat on the deck and talked about Paris. I think she's making decisions."

"How do you mean?"

"Moving her out of that house has had an effect. She may not go back."

"Because of Eden?"

"No. Because she wants to try something different. One thing's clear, Jimmy—she's tired of being pushed around."

"I'll do my best to stop the ones pushing."

"I'm sure you will. Mary's worth the effort, Jimmy. I like her."

After we'd hung up I sat in bed with my drink and the book I'd stolen from Sam and read about Hemingway's early years in Paris. I fell asleep while reading, but didn't dream about Paris, or Hemingway, or Eden Development. I dreamed that Dana McOscar and I were flying in a small plane. We took off through a curtain of tree branches and cruised to a summer lake lit up blue and white in hot sunlight. We made passes at the lake, letting the landing gear just touch the surface.

CHAPTER ELEVEN

Fishing
for Shark

At NINE-THIRTY the next morning I got off the elevator on the thirtieth floor of a downtown office building and lied to the receptionist at Amory & Harcourt. I told her I had an appointment with George Amory. She got me seated with a cup of coffee and a copy of *The Wall Street Journal,* then spent a minute on the phone before she turned and said politely, "Are you sure your appointment was with Mr. George Amory?"

"Tell him I'm a representative of Eden Development."

She told him, listened for a moment, then hung up. "Someone will be right along," she said. A few minutes later a gray-haired woman came for me. She led me up a spiral staircase and down a long corridor of offices overlooking Boston Harbor. We went all the way to the end of the corridor, to a corner room with views of both the harbor and the Charles River basin. The room had two hundred square feet of woven wool rug on the floor, showing a stylized figure, half bird, half man, grasping two smaller figures. The walls were hung with oil paintings of the old West, and a cacti garden grew in the corner window. I half expected to find J. R. Ewing grinning at me from under the brim of a ten-gallon hat, but the nameplate outside the door said WILLIAM AMORY. My escort stopped just inside the office, said my name, and left me to confront father and son.

George sat in a sand-colored armchair by the window on the harbor side. He opened his mouth in surprise when he saw me.

Amory Senior was behind an oak and stainless steel desk, with a view of distant sailboats framed by the window behind him. They both wore green suspenders with matching bow ties, but the father had his sleeves rolled up. If not for his short, iron-gray hair, Bill Amory could have passed for a man of forty. He looked like the type who jogs ten miles every morning wearing leg weights, comes home to a carefully monitored high-fiber breakfast, and drives his Mercedes to work with one hand, so he can squeeze rubber balls with the other. I'd have bet his handshake would be extra manly, but he didn't offer it.

He said, "Close the door."

George said, "He's been following me, Dad. He was at the Parker House last night."

"What the hell is this about? Who are you?"

I took a seat in a leather director's chair opposite the desk. The wall to my left was dominated by an oak and glass case full of antique guns. The centerpiece of the collection was a brace of pearl-handled Colt .45s in studded leather holsters. I wondered if Bill ever took them out and strapped them on—maybe when he was alone at night, when he could see his reflection in the big windows. I said, "My name is Mallory. I'm from Eden Development."

"That's what you told the receptionist. It's bullshit. Tell us who you are and what you want or get out."

I thought it was interesting that he was so sure I wasn't from Eden—if he knew as little about his client as he'd led Michael to believe, he had no reason to think I was lying. I ignored the father and turned to the son, who looked scared. I said, "Who hired you to represent Eden Development, George?"

The father picked up his phone and said into the mouthpiece, "Edith, get security."

I smiled across at him. "Maybe I'm not from Eden. Maybe I'm from the IRS."

"The IRS would call my secretary and ask for an appointment. Politely. I don't know what your game is, Mallory, and I don't care. You give me a good reason to listen to you, or when the security guards get here you're out on your butt."

"You're a tough hombre, aren't you? Harvey Blackstone told me you'd listen." George reacted to that—he sat up straighter in his chair and looked across at his father. Bill pretended not to notice him. It made me almost feel sorry for George—he seemed completely out of place in that office full of sublimated aggressions, like a goldfish sharing a bowl with a piranha.

The father said, "Get back to work, George. I'll handle this."

George gave me a nasty look on his way out. I said, "I guess Harvey's name was good enough to keep me here."

"You guessed wrong. Just about every lawyer in this town has a piece of Harvey Blackstone's legal business, and I'd listen to any representative he sent to me. But Harvey doesn't send me representatives, he comes himself. I think I can guess who you're really working for. Michael Garrison is trying his best to find out about Eden Development. I've cooperated with him to the extent I could without violating the confidentiality of a former client's affairs. That's all I have to say to either you or Michael. In deference to him, I'm giving you the opportunity to walk out of here without an escort."

"If Harvey Blackstone's the man behind Eden," I said, "and he's using the partnership to launder unreported income, then you'll end up walking out of here under the escort of federal marshalls. You'll be an accessory to tax fraud. A criminal."

Bill looked as if he wanted to belt me, but got control of his dignity and decided to hit me with precepts instead of fists. He pointed to his collection of firearms and said, "The guns in that case are antiques, Mr. Mallory, but each one is fully functional, and I keep them loaded. Like those guns, there is nothing in my character that is bluff. When I make a threat, I mean it, and I'm fully capable of executing it. You stay away from my son and this firm or I'll have your balls."

I thought to myself, You played it wrong, Bill. Bland innocence would have been better. Two security guards stepped into the room and looked to Amory for instructions. I smiled at them, got up, and left the office.

I found my way back to the receptionist, with the security guards following twenty paces behind. They let me get on the elevator alone. I'd wanted to provoke a reaction, but I hadn't expected quite so much hoopla. Maybe the hoopla wasn't a sign of guilty knowledge, maybe it was only a characteristic response from Bill Amory—he was clearly a man who resorted to browbeating by instinct.

It had been a short visit, and now it was a quick ride to the street. In the time it would take me to stroll down to Harvey Blackstone's office on the waterfront, however, Bill or George would have more than enough opportunity to get on the phone and warn Harvey that I'd be coming. I'd be curious to see whether he was prepared for me.

Blackstone's office was in a rehabilitated warehouse on one of the old landfill piers projecting from the North End's waterfront. The building was as solid as the Boston businessmen who'd built it two centuries ago, made from giant blocks of granite. The blocks had been cut at intervals now, for installation of floor-to-ceiling windows. The windows looked out on a small marina full of sailboats and cabin cruisers and a patch of fenced lawn and Oriental cherry trees that seemed out of place on a spit of manmade land flanked by salt water.

A private elevator ran up to Blackstone's lobby, where I found yet another bored receptionist and a guy who looked like a bouncer at a wet T-shirt contest. The bouncer sat on a leather couch against one wall, reading *Time* magazine. He could have been a client, but I guessed Harvey had got a phone call after all, and he was there for my benefit.

I ignored him and headed into a corridor that ran behind the receptionist's desk. She said, "Hey!" I kept going, came across a second desk with a secretary outside an office door.

I said, "Mr. Blackstone?" She didn't answer, so I went in. A bullet-headed guy in a charcoal-gray suit looked up from behind a mahogany desk where he was trying to get a tiny wooden ship through the mouth of a plain glass bottle.

I shut the door and turned the dead-bolt lock. The walls of the office were hung with harpoons, brass chronometers, and dead fish. In half a dozen glass display cases large-scale wooden models of three-masters stood under full sail. There were displays of carved whalebone and other artifacts that sea captains used to collect when they journeyed around the horn to China— blue porcelain vases, carved ivory palaces, and fans. Apparently Harvey Blackstone, like Bill Amory, liked a personalized working environment.

Somebody rattled the door at my back and I said, "Potential energy."

"What the fuck's going on?"

"When objects fall, their potential energy is converted into kinetic energy, which is what could happen to the objects in this room if you don't call off your man."

He frowned, reached for the telephone on the desk, hit a button, and said, "Tell Matt to forget it." The rattling at the door stopped. Blackstone looked at me and said, "What the fuck do you want?"

I sat in one of the brown leather chairs arranged in front of the desk. "I'm a private investigator. I'm here about Eden Development."

He put aside the ship and bottle. "I have absolutely no interest in Eden Development. They beat me to the brass ring on a very sweet deal, and since then I've tried to put them out of my mind. So you can leave."

"I understood you and Eden are one and the same."

"You understood wrong."

"I bet you own a lot of companies that nobody knows about, companies you control from behind the scenes. Like South End Realty."

"You're way off. I've never heard of them—which means they must be small potatoes."

I stared at him for a full minute, hoping he'd feel the compulsion to say more. He matched my silence, but he also didn't ask me to leave. I got up and walked around the desk to look at a framed photograph of a boat on the wall behind him. He swiveled his chair to watch me. I said, "It's an Alden forty-four, isn't it? Beautiful boat."

"You sail?"

"I sometimes crew for a friend."

"If you look out that window you can see that same boat down in the marina. I'm this city's biggest property owner, but I don't give a shit about land. It brings me money, that's all. Whenever I have the opportunity, I sail." He smiled a small, tight-lipped smile. "I'm like those guys with the bumper stickers—I'd rather be sailing."

"Some of your tenants wish you'd spend all your time at sea. Without a boat."

"So now you want to provoke a reaction, is that it? What is it you really want from me, Mallory?"

I registered the fact that he knew my name, though I hadn't

given it. "Just to deliver a message. The people who live at Eden's Garden aren't going to give up. They've got money behind them now, and lawyers."

He snorted. "And they're low income to boot, right? They probably want Eden to put Jacuzzis in their fucking bathrooms so they can make more babies. I've never given a shit about tenants either. No matter what you give them, they always want more. But if Eden's having problems, I'm glad. They skunked me."

"I wouldn't think anybody could skunk Harvey Blackstone when it came to real estate."

"Eden had that touch of magic known as ready cash. I couldn't match their offer."

"Did you make any effort to approach them?"

"Once they made that deal, I made no effort to find them. Why should I? I didn't get rich crying over spilled milk. I assure you, you're on the wrong track. Now if you'll excuse me, I got work to do." He picked up the model ship he'd been trying to get into the bottle. He didn't smile.

"Maybe the newspapers would be interested in your connection to Eden," I said. "Or the IRS."

"I'm already the most hated man in this town, and the IRS audits me every year like clockwork."

"It's difficult to audit cash receipts," I said. "Unless you know where the money's hidden."

"That's enough, Mr. Mallory." This time he buzzed his secretary. "I've given you the grand total of my knowledge on the subject of Eden Development, and of my patience. You tell tales behind my back, watch yourself. I got lawyers too."

The door opened with a key and Matt stood on the sill like Samson getting ready to pull down the temple.

"If anything happens to anyone living on that block, and I find out you're responsible, I'm going to come back here and put that harpoon through your liver," I said.

He smiled, this time looking like one of the sharks that cruise the walls of the big tank at the aquarium. I got up to leave and Matt blocked my way. Harvey said, "Throw him out, Matthew. And don't be gentle."

Matthew grabbed my shoulders. I brought my knee up and hit him in the groin. He dropped his hands to hold himself, and I gave him a shove that sent him back into the corridor. I headed for the lobby, not rushing it, but skipped the elevator and used the stairs. I made it down to the street without any interference.

At the Trojan there was a brief message from Michael: "What the hell's happening?"

I called, and before I could get beyond hello he repeated the question. "Caroline's been calling every half hour, absolutely hysterical. Mary's disappeared."

"I disappeared her, Michael." And I explained the events of the previous evening. "I don't want to tell you where she is. She'll be safer that way. You can tell Caroline you don't know where, but she's okay."

"She'll never buy that, but I'll live with it. Are you making any progress?"

"I've been gate-crashing." I told him about my meetings with the Amorys and Blackstone. "Wild Bill Amory is a bull, it's hard to tell what's motivating him. Everything Blackstone told me was plausible, but the question remains, why did he go to so much trouble to convince me? When I pressed him about unreported income, he threw me out. And somebody called to let him know I was coming."

"I still find it hard to believe a guy like Bill Amory would get involved in a mess like this."

"Then maybe it's George acting on his own initiative. Or

maybe it's neither, and I'm completely off base. I'll work on it. In the meantime, try to keep Caroline off my back."

After we hung up I called to check in with Mangenello. I got him on the first ring.

"I tried to reach you," he said, "but I got that damned answering machine."

"What's up?"

"I told you I'd be creative," he said. "I got the FBI and DEA sitting here. They want to talk with you about Eden Development."

I told him I'd be right over.

CHAPTER TWELVE

Just
Say No

I STEPPED INTO a room full of cops. It was hot, the air conditioning was on the blink, but Simon looked cool as a cucumber in a heavy wool suit. His two guests were in short sleeves and sweating. One of them I recognized—Harold Peters, head of the local FBI unit. He looked like an aging astronaut, with a 1950s crew cut and a square, freshly shaved jaw. The other guy was younger, with a deep tan and longish black hair.

Simon said, "Long time no see, Mallory. You know Harold. This is Joe Mariosa, Drug Enforcement Agency, out of Miami."

Mariosa gave me a look of appraisal, then reached to shake hands. Peters scowled and said, "We're still looking for your buddy Frank Burger."

I smiled. Frank was a close friend, a lawyer who'd absconded with six million dollars in clients' funds several years back and hadn't been seen since. I'd gone off to Europe at about the same time, and the FBI had been convinced I was Frank's accomplice. For several months afterward they'd dogged my footsteps, waiting for the inevitable rendezvous that never came. I said, "As you can see, I still haven't retired on my ill-gotten gains."

Peters's jaw got squarer, and Mangenello said, "Never mind that crap, we got business."

I sat down across from Simon and asked, "Why's DEA interested in Eden Development?"

Mariosa leaned forward and said, "Jack Eden."

"It was the money laundering got me thinking," Simon said with a small, gratified smile. "For the past few years a lot of drug money has been slipping into the Northeast. My inquiry to DEA's computer got an unexpected priority."

"You're looking for the man behind Eden Development," Mariosa told me. "I'm looking for a man named Jack Eden, wanted for drug smuggling and arson. I think we're after the same guy."

"So tell me about him."

He reached into a file on the edge of Simon's desk, handed me a photograph of a blond man, in his late thirties, handsome in a generic, American way. He was dressed like a lawyer in a blue summer suit and yellow tie. He'd spotted the camera and was waving and smiling in an exaggerated way. The photo was labeled on the back JACK EDEN.

"Never saw him before."

"Keep the photo, you may need it," Mariosa said. "Eden ran an operation out of South Florida for two years, bringing cocaine in from Colombia. Up until this spring he lived aboard a fifty-four-foot cabin cruiser tied up at a marina in Fort Lauderdale. In April we were on the verge of closing down his operation—we had warrants and were ready to go in—when he took his boat out for a cruise. Half an hour later the boat exploded and burned to the waterline."

"But Eden wasn't aboard?"

Mariosa nodded and reached for more photos, eight-by-ten glossies, which he held facedown in his lap. "We were meant to think he was," he said. "Our agent watching the boat got these shots—telephoto lens, so they're grainy." He handed me the first of the series and kept his eyes on my face. It showed a big cabin cruiser plowing down the inland waterway on a sunny Florida day. It looked sleek enough to be fast in the water, but with a wide beam to allow for lots of living space. Custom made, at least five hundred grand. There was a man at its helm, too far away to identify.

Mariosa seemed to expect some response, so I said, "Nice boat."

"Very posh inside. The lounge was done up like an English study, with walnut bookcases and leather armchairs. Registered out of Fort Lauderdale. You know how people give their boats cutsie names, like the *Freudian Sloop,* that kind of thing? You can't see the transom in these photos, but right across the stern, in big gold letters, you'd see the name for this rig: *Just Say No.*"

I smiled. "Not ashamed of his source of income," I said. "Kind of like Dow Chemical naming the corporate boat the *Napalmed Baby.*"

Peters snorted indignantly and shifted in his chair, Simon gave a little chuckle, and Mariosa looked at me closely. Then he smiled. "Just about as shocking." He handed me the next four photos without any preamble—the *Just Say No* passing behind a dredging barge, emerging from the other side—then in the third, the first red flare of an explosion, shooting out from under the cockpit where the man was standing. In the last photo there was nothing but a ball of intense yellow flame and flying debris. They were the kind of photos *Life* magazine loves to publish and would probably pay a fortune for.

"What makes you think Eden's still alive?" I said. "The guy at the helm isn't."

"The guy at the helm never was." Mariosa handed over the last photo from the stack. All three cops watched me closely. The photo was an enlargement of the cockpit of the *Just Say No* as it emerged from behind the barge—and there was the punchline. It showed a blurred close-up of the man at the helm, not Eden, but old Ronald Reagan himself. I blinked and took a closer look—it was the Gipper all right, a two-dimensional, life-sized figure, the kind of cardboard cutout tourists pose beside on the Mall in Washington.

"Ha-ha," I said. Mariosa still watched me, one eyebrow raised. "Okay, so I'm surprised. What's your point?"

"Eden got the word we were going to bust him, that's clear. He must have had a dinghy tied off on the starboard side, or maybe his partner was waiting behind the barge with a boat. He propped the cardboard figure at the helm and bailed out. I guess I'm trying to enlist you, Mallory. And I want you to understand Eden the way I do."

"He went to all that trouble to fake his death," I said, "but he must have known the boat was under observation—must have counted on it. The cardboard figure was a message."

"Now you've got it. He faked his death, but he left behind that cardboard dummy so we'd *know* he faked his death. Not a message, necessarily, just a joke. Eden's like that—unpredictable, inventive, loony."

"Mr. Good Time."

"Right. To give you the full picture, I'd need to show you snapshots of fifteen-year-old kids dead from cocaine Eden brought into the country. But I figure you know about that kind of thing."

"I can do without the snapshots. But why the practical joke?"

"To make DEA look bad."

"That's a lot of boat to waste on something the media does for free."

Mariosa grimaced. "To you and me it is. It's one of the problems we run into in this business. Eden had been smuggling cocaine for two years when the *Just Say No* blew up, and he was big time almost from the start. People in that league keep money in suitcases. They can pay cops double their annual salaries in bribes and not feel it. They can use an expensive boat for one run to Colombia, then deep-six it. Eden probably has forty million stashed away in accounts in the Cayman Islands. And that's a conservative estimate."

I handed back the photos. "So what's the connection to real estate in Boston—other than the name? There must be a thousand Edens in this town."

"First, we know he's probably hiding out in the Northeast, on a farm somewhere. For two years he's been telling people that's what he'd do when he retired, live off the land, like Thoreau. Second, laundering drug money in real estate makes sense— Eden's not the type to let his cash sit in a numbered account. Finally, there's the style of this enterprise, as you described it to Captain Mangenello. My instinct tells me it's Jack Eden. It smells like him."

"Instinct," Peters muttered, but Mariosa ignored him, fixing his eyes on me, waiting for the next question.

"You mentioned a partner."

He nodded. "Another point. The Hispanic accent of the person who made the threatening calls to your client. The partner's a Colombian: Jorge Varega."

He handed me another photo. Varega was short, dark, and stocky, with thick forearms and powerful-looking hands. Someone you wouldn't want to meet in a dark alley.

"You can keep that photo too," Mariosa said. "Varega disappeared in April, just after Eden. We've never known much about him, except he's reputed to have killed his first two partners. The type of man Eden would choose, just for the hell of it."

The air conditioner came on with a clatter, and three of us looked at it gratefully.

"This isn't the guy who broke into Mary's place," I said. "Different body type."

"It wouldn't be—Varega's a rich man. But he often works with other Colombians."

"What are the chances Eden might be involved in a partner-ship with local people?" I said.

Mariosa nodded. "I know what you're getting at. Captain Mangenello told me you suspected a man named Blackstone might be behind Eden Development."

"Blackstone's legit," Peters interrupted. "I know that for a fact."

"It's not inconceivable that Eden would have a local con-nection," Mariosa went on. "We know nothing about his life prior to the day he arrived in Miami on a flight from Colombia two and a half years ago. Customs wasn't able to find any record of a prior departure from the States. Probably bought his passport in Colombia."

"You must really be hot for this guy," I said, "to have men watching that private mailbox service just three hours after I spoke with Simon."

Mariosa nodded again. All that approval was probably de-signed to make me lower my guard, give out more information than I intended—not that I had much to give at that point. "Peters assigned two men as soon as we heard about Eden Develop-ment," Mariosa said. "They've now been replaced by DEA agents. You probably won't spot my men as easily."

"I've had enough of this shit," Peters said, but he didn't get up and leave, and Mariosa continued to ignore him. Interdepart-mental rivalry is a wonderful thing—keeps America strong.

"Why are you putting such a high priority on tracking down a man who's obviously retired from the trade?" I asked.

Mariosa leaned forward, looking intense and serious. I don't think he was faking it. "It's bad enough when people call us corrupt," he said. "We're used to that, the press has been bash-ing us for years, and to some extent they're justified. But Eden got a lot of people laughing at us. People like Peters here have less respect for us. I want Eden. I don't want to think of him thumbing his nose at DEA and then retiring to live in a villa in the south of France, all because I couldn't do my job."

I thought that Mariosa must be good at his job if he was able to call up all that support from DEA for what looked like a grudge match. "Have your men taken a look at the records of that private mail service?" I asked.

"We don't have enough evidence to support a warrant."

"The mail sent to box 331 gets forwarded to another P.O. box—in Miami." I gave him the address and number.

"You burgled that place," Peters growled at me. "If my agents got caught doing that kind of thing, you'd be the first one out on the streets protesting."

I wondered if he was making an obscure reference to some material he'd read in my secret FBI file. Mariosa snapped at him, "That's exactly the kind of information we hoped to get from Mr. Mallory." To me he said, "My team will check out that address. I'd appreciate anything else you can give me."

I turned to Mangenello. "How do you fit into this, Simon?"

"You got me into it. I'm here to introduce you fellows and provide a room to talk in. And if it's drug money coming across our borders, the Commonwealth would be interested. I'll be glad to serve as your communication center."

I said to Mariosa, "Okay, I'm enlisted. I can't say you've convinced me we're looking for the same guy, but if I come up with anything that points to Jack Eden, I'll let you know. Hopefully you'll reciprocate."

"Of course," Mariosa told me. "That goes without saying."

As I got up to leave Peters said, "We'll be watching you, Mallory."

CHAPTER THIRTEEN

What's in a Name?

I MADE SIX PHONE CALLS that Wednesday night. I called Michael to report on my latest development, which left him properly confused. The problem with Jack Eden as a suspect was his motivation—I doubted that he'd buy Eden's Garden for anything but laundering illicit funds, and if that was the case, why call attention to himself by bashing tenants? Even if he was unpredictable, inventive, and loony, it didn't make sense. It made more sense that Blackstone, or some other local real estate tycoon, was using the blind partnership as a mechanism to avoid service of process—so she or he could bash tenants with impunity. But why was mail being forwarded to Miami?

Michael didn't have the answers. He had checked out Caroline's Winfred, though. Mary's nephew-in-law owned a city block in the South End, not far from University Hospital, but it was managed by a real estate firm that happened to be Michael's client.

"They're legit as they come," Michael said. "More like a trust company than a developer. I'd say Winfred wasn't much of a suspect."

"We've got too many suspects now anyway," I told him. "I'll keep you posted."

My next call was to another old friend, Baldo Carlucci, who writes freelance for some of the big-name magazines. He'd re-

cently done an article on drug trafficking in South Florida. I got
Baldo's answering machine and left a message asking him to call
back.

Then I called Jay to find out if there'd been any developments in Maine. There hadn't been. "I think Cross is waiting for
the first snow to drive Hank out of the woods," he told me.

We kicked around various things he might try, in the way of
investigation. All we came up with was that he'd check the registry
of deeds to see if there was any basis for Clive Linscott's claim that
Ben had been cutting on Clive's land the day he was killed.

Phone call number four was to Barbi. She told me Mary was
doing fine, but sleeping. I told her about Jack Eden, and she
didn't have any answers either. She'd made a few discreet inquiries about Harvey Blackstone, but came up with nothing.

I hesitated before calling Dana McOscar, and when I did
there was no answer. So I walked alone out Beacon Street to
Coolidge Corner and saw Alfred Hitchcock's *Notorious,* with
Cary Grant and Ingrid Bergman. The opening scenes are set in
Miami in the 1950s, the cinematography is black and white, but
the movie's palm trees against moonlit skies are more luminous
and romantic than any full-color picture postcard. I thought about
flying down to Miami, to see what information I could dig up on
Jack Eden. I decided to sleep on it.

When I got home to Marlborough Street, I called Della to
check for messages. There was one from Phil Levine, left earlier
that evening. The old man who'd lived at Eden's Garden, the one
who'd been badly beaten about the same time Mary was attacked
and who'd been in the hospital ever since, had died.

At eleven the next morning I hiked across Boston Common,
headed for Beacon Hill and Pemberton Square. Dana had
called—Judge Chapman wanted to see me.

I climbed the steps to the courthouse and made it through the metal detector, then waited five minutes for one of the anachronistic, manually operated elevators to arrive. Finally an old crate jammed to a stop in the lobby. I got in, said "Thirteen," and the operator—a thin guy, about five feet tall—leaned on the brass lever and shot us up to the Supreme Judicial Court of Massachusetts.

Two security guards lounged at a desk outside the suite of judges' chambers. One was stocky and balding, the other had thick, wavy hair and resembled Clark Gable. Both carried .38s in hip holsters, and both looked like they hadn't shot anyone for a long time and could use a break in routine. I identified myself and the older guard led me down to Judge Chapman.

The Judge was behind his desk, lounging back in a leather and oak swivel chair, rocking the chair slowly from side to side. His eyes were closed and he held one hand to his forehead, meditatively. There was a burning cigarette in that hand. Dana sat attentively in the chair beside his desk, her hair tied back in a loose ponytail, wearing a long print dress. The dress was pretty and old-fashioned-looking. She seemed to be waiting for the Judge to make up his mind about something. He opened his eyes, saw me, and smiled.

"We'll figure this out later," he said to Dana. She saw me at the door and also smiled.

"Come in, Mr. Mallory," the Judge said, transferring the cigarette to his left hand and stretching his right out to shake, without leaning forward in the chair. His thinness shocked me. When I'd known him at Harvard he'd been a powerful man in his fifties, someone who played tennis every afternoon and took pleasure in beating the daylights out of men in their twenties. Now he'd dropped at least fifty pounds. But his handshake was still strong.

I said, "I'm surprised you recognize me after all these years, Judge."

"I never forget the names and faces of my former students. You were great friends with Jay Franklin—still are, I understand. That's why you were in Maine when my brother died. We buried him yesterday." He took a drag at his cigarette, then stubbed it out in a dirty ashtray. I couldn't tell by his expression whether he was saddened by his brother's death or indifferent. Maybe after ten years on the bench he'd gotten used to hiding any personal reaction to tragedy, and the habit had carried over into his private life.

I took a seat by his desk and looked around the room. There were bookshelves lining every wall, and a stack of what looked like unbound galley proofs on a big oak table, which probably meant the Judge was about to bring out another edition of his famous treatise on contracts. The only window in the room was medium size, set too high in the wall to offer a view. On the few square feet of wall not covered by books, beside the window, a cheap poster had been tacked up with red thumbtacks. It said, in black calligraphy across a pink background, JUST BECAUSE YOU'RE PARANOID DOESN'T MEAN THEY AREN'T OUT TO GET YOU.

The Judge smiled again. "Dana said you wanted to ask me questions about my brother, Ben."

"I thought you wanted to see me," I told him.

"That's true also. I was curious to hear your conclusions. I've been working to put Ben's affairs in order."

"I understand he left everything to you."

"He didn't have a will, but yes, I was his only living relative. He left nothing to Hank Tuttle, if that's the question behind your question. Even if he had, Hank wouldn't get it. The law says you can't inherit from a man you've murdered. For obvious reasons."

"Are you convinced Hank Tuttle's a murderer?"

"That's why I asked you here. To find out what you think."

"I'm flattered, but I have no basis for reaching any con-
clusion."

Dana leaned back in her chair and looked at me through
narrowed eyes. The Judge coughed, then grimaced as if in pain.
"Dana tells me otherwise, but I see you've retained one habit
from your short-lived career in law. You don't like to commit
yourself to any point of view. I had to change all that around
when I became a judge. People expect us to give answers without
equivocation. Though some of my colleagues often ignore that
golden rule."

"What do you think about Hank?"

He sat up in his chair to get a cigarette, took a moment to
light it with a brass Zippo lighter. "Flight is considered an admission of guilt in a court of law," he said at last. "Hank fled."

"But you have doubts?"

"I want to be fair. I've known Hank from his childhood. But
if you accept his hypothetical innocence, you have the problem of
finding someone else with a motive. There's me, of course, since
I inherited. I'd have had some trouble with the physical require-
ments of such a task, but I could have hired someone to handle
the actual murder." He looked at his smoking cigarette and
frowned. "I might even have hired Hank."

Dana sat watching him closely, and when he looked up he
met her eyes only briefly, then turned back to the smoking cigarette. He took a long drag and blew the smoke out through his
nostrils. The thought of all that poison going into his fragile lungs
made me wince.

I said, "I've heard Ben came close to breaking the law in
some of his business deals and that you took care of little problems for him. Like fixing things with the local D.A." Dana shot
me a quick, angry look, but I went on. "Could that have been a
source of other motives?"

"I won't ask who gave you that misinformation. The fact

that it was given—and I believe I know the source—is an indication of bad feelings that go back a long time and have nothing to do with business. My brother was respected as a businessman. Chapman is an old English word that means 'trader,' and that's what my brother was, an old Yankee trader. Of course, it's possible that someone who got the short end of a deal with him may have resented that. It's also possible that someone like that might have killed him."

"What makes you think it wasn't Hank?"

The Judge went on as if he hadn't heard me. "Chapman is an honored name in Sangerville. We were original settlers there, almost two hundred years ago."

"Judge," Dana said softly, "do you know anything that might help Hank?"

"I'm sorry," he said. "I got you here on false pretenses, Mr. Mallory, since I'm not yet prepared to share my thoughts on the matter. I hoped you might have some ideas."

"I was told that the land Ben was killed on belonged to Clive Linscott. That Ben was stealing timber."

The Judge shook his head and frowned. "Clive is not always accurate on such matters. He shared Ben's passion for land, and at times that led them to disputes. I sometimes acted to resolve the disputes, because I'm a lawyer. That particular piece of land was the subject of litigation many years ago, and Clive has never reconciled himself to its loss."

"So much so that he might have killed your brother?"

"I doubt it. As I said, the litigation was resolved years ago, and it was not unusual for Linscott to engage in such disputes. I understand he spends a great deal of time in court, often complaining about people cutting his timber. He's paranoid, Mr. Mallory."

He stubbed out the cigarette. "The fact is, I've had a personal report from the local D.A. The evidence against Hank suggests a strong possibility of guilt. Perhaps your investigation will produce contrary evidence—I hope so. But that's all I have to say for the moment."

"Judge . . ." Dana said.

"I'm lunching at the club," he interrupted her, and said to me, "Every Thursday I engage in a very old-fashioned male ritual, eating lunch with ten elderly and distinguished members of the bar in a club that, until recently, did not admit women, blacks, or Jews. Then I come back to the court and write my opinions dealing with the constitutional rights of women and minorities. That makes me a hypocrite. If you'll excuse me, Mr. Mallory." He pried himself out of the swivel chair, went to a rack behind the door, and took down a suit jacket. He shrugged it over his shoulders and left.

Dana turned to me and said, "What do you mean you have no basis for thinking Hank's innocent?"

"Or guilty," I said. "You know the Judge better than I do. Is he holding back something?"

She frowned. "Something's bothering him. This morning he asked me to do some research on Maine law—then before I could leave the room he told me to forget it."

"Research on what issue?"

"Champerty. I had to look it up in *Black's Law Dictionary.* It's an old-fashioned concept. It's when people do title searches to find weaknesses in the chain of title to a piece of property, then buy out the conflicting interest and threaten the owner in possession with litigation—usually to squeeze a piece of land out of them. It's illegal. It's like extortion, a criminal offense."

"Maybe somebody's holding a deed against one of Ben's properties."

"Could be."

"Think you could find out?"

"I'll ask the Judge if he needs any help with the estate documents, but I think he's doing it all at home. Did you get the feeling he wants to be convinced Hank killed Ben?"

"Like it would simplify things if Hank were guilty? How does that make you feel?"

"Rotten. But we've never discussed the fact that Hank's my brother. Not after I'd told the Judge I knew I was adopted, not once during this last year when I've worked with him every day. When I talk to him about Hank, he barely listens."

"People are funny," I said.

"Knowing that doesn't help me, Mallory. And it doesn't help Hank."

CHAPTER FOURTEEN

The Sisyphus Fan Club

I LEFT DANA WORKING on the Judge's galley proofs and spent the rest of the afternoon checking in with various contacts, trying to find a cocaine connection to either Harvey Blackstone or George Amory. As far as I was able to determine, there wasn't any. Just after five I checked in at the Trojan and took a long swim in the twenty-five-meter pool. I was showered and feeling well exercised when I tried Baldo again from my office phone. This time his answering machine had a special message for me: "Mallory, stop calling every five minutes! I'm going to a Red Sox game. I'll be outside the Cask and Flagon."

It was typical of Baldo to leave a message on his own machine, rather than bothering to call me. It fit in with his solipsistic worldview, which probably derives from the fact that Baldo is big enough to be a planet in his own right.

I took the subway to Kenmore Square. I hadn't been to a Red Sox game since they lost the series in '86, and, crossing the bridge over the turnpike, I realized I'd missed them. The usual pregame crowd swarmed outside the park—fans, pennant sellers, hot dog vendors, and ticket scalpers.

The Cask and Flagon is in the center of all the action, on the corner of Landsdowne Street. If you spend the last half hour before a game waiting on that corner, you can peruse anywhere from ten to thirty thousand profiles. I once bet a friend fifty bucks he couldn't do it without running into somebody he didn't want to

see. He ran into his ex-wife. They subsequently reconciled and remarried.

Baldo was on his way out of the bar when I arrived, all three hundred pounds of him, his face flushed with drinking and his pale-blue eyes blinking against the sunlight. Despite his nickname, he's not bald—Baldo is short for Balder, the Norse god of light, peace, and virtue—or so he tells me. He spotted me and grinned.

"I owe you money, right? I always forget things like that, but I'll gladly pay you Tuesday. How are you, Jimmy?"

"Five beers behind you. I want to pick your brain."

"Sounds disgusting. It'll cost you the price of admission to the bleachers. What do you wanna know about?"

"Jack Eden. If you don't know him, you'll have to buy your own ticket."

"Know him? I'm writing a fucking book about the guy. Come on." And he started to muscle his way through the crowd. He moved like an ambulance in rush-hour traffic. Baldo's bulk is accentuated by the fact that he's only five six—but it's not all fat, he works out every day at the B.U. gym.

I followed him to the ticket booth behind the left-field wall and bought two general admissions to the bleachers. Once under the stands we bought beer and hot dogs, then stepped out into the sunlight. I looked across the field to the diamond and the net behind home plate and the fans moving about looking for seats, heard the hokey sound of the pregame organ music, and my belly went hollow with excitement. We sat in the very last row of unreserved seats, under the giant electronic scoreboard.

"My favorite seats in the house," Baldo said. "When I sit up here, I feel like the whole goddamn stadium is watching me."

"Tell me about Jack Eden."

"I ran into all kinds of crazy people down in Florida, but

Eden was one of the craziest. I wasn't kidding, I wanna write a book about the guy. Maybe you got something I can use?"

"How about a connection to Boston?" I told him about Eden Development and my contact with Mariosa, the DEA agent. I was interrupted by the national anthem. Then I told him about the explosion on the *Just Say No* and the Ronald Reagan cutout. He tore his eyes from the field and grinned at me. "I'd heard about the explosion, of course, but not the bit about old Ronnie. I'd give a thousand bucks for a copy of that picture."

"I'll see what I can do."

"Mariosa's talking through his hat when he says they were ready to bust Eden. They'd been trying to do that for two years and never got close. Not that Eden didn't give them plenty of opportunity."

"How so?"

"According to legend—and this is a man about whom there are legends—Eden called DEA before every big drop and challenged them to a game of hide and seek. The Coast Guard doubled their coverage, and he'd slip through. Then he'd throw a big party to celebrate and invite all the local law enforcement jocks. He liked a good joke."

"If DEA wasn't closing in on him, why'd he pull the disappearing act?"

"Some say he wanted to retire, live on a farm somewhere. I heard he stole three million bucks from his partner."

"Varega?"

"You got it. The fact that Varega disappeared at the same time lends some credence to that theory. He's not the type you'd want to steal anything from—mean son of a bitch, believes the only way to right a wrong is to chop somebody's head off. He's famous in the trade too. One guy he went after, he missed on the first try. Guy hired bodyguards. A year later, when the bodyguards left, Varega came back and cut out his liver. Had it delivered to the widow on the day of the funeral. That's probably an apocryphal story, but you get the point. If he was looking for me, I'd run too."

"If he caught up with Eden and found out his money was invested in Boston real estate, what do you think he'd do?"

"After he got done roasting Eden's *cojones*? He'd do whatever it took to get his money back. Not that he really needs it, but he'd have to prove he hadn't been taken. You end up messing with that guy, Jimmy, make sure you watch your back."

Parrish hit a long, hard drive that went off the left-field wall and the crowd was on its feet. "Let's see what they do with a base runner on second and no outs," Baldo said.

What they did was go down one, two, three, leaving Parrish stranded.

"Eden's pretty vindictive himself," Baldo said. "Left some surprises for a few people in South Florida when he took off. Local politician had a habit of telling the press Jack was a blackguard. Guy was playing the war-on-drugs game for all it was worth. A week after the *Just Say No* blew up, the Miami papers got eight-by-ten glossies of the politician snorting coke in a bathroom stall. Eden had personally autographed each of the glossies."

"Where were the photos mailed from?"

"No clue for you there, Jimmy. They were sent out in the politician's own envelopes, metered by the guy's own office machine, as campaign mail. Some joke, heh? About the same time Eden's biggest competitor got a package in the mail. They'd been cutting into each other's territory for two years, hated each other's guts. Guess what was in the package?"

"A bomb?"

"Close enough. Videotape of the guy's wife in the sack with

his right-hand man. Eden had had a fight with the lover boy once, at a party. So he killed two birds with one stone."

"Where'd you get all this information?"

"Sources. Woodward and Bernstein ain't got nothin' on me. Like I say, I'm writing a book. And believe me, the book ain't going to be critical of Eden. I don't want to wake up some morning and find a scorpion in my boots. He's one of those funny types with absolutely no sense of humor about themselves."

"You know Mariosa at all?"

"I interviewed him once. His father brought the family from Cuba after Fidel took over, and the father's still working to oust the commies. Mariosa's not as conservative as his old man, but he's fanatical about his work—gets a lot accomplished too, considering the degree of corruption in local officials and the sheer volume of trade down there. It's like the gold rush, Jimmy."

"Has any of the corruption hit Mariosa?"

"I think he'd die before he'd take a bribe. Decent guy. Got a beautiful wife and two kids. Eden was his first real failure. I'd say if he had the chance, he'd challenge him to a duel at high noon, outside the Fontainbleu, and to hell with due process."

"What are you going to call your book?" I asked him.

"*Eden in Paradise*. Not bad, heh? Anyway, we're missing the game. I think these guys have a chance this year."

"I can't stay. After eighty-six I've got permanent psychological scars."

"To forgive is divine, Jimmy. How long were you a fan—twenty, thirty years? Think of it as a privilege, being a member of the Sisyphus Fan Club. They keep rolling the rock up the hill, and when they get near the top we yell so loud, they get disconcerted and let go of the damned rock. Read about it in *Sports Illustrated*. I'm writing an article for them."

It had gotten dark, and the stadium lights glowed above the

stands while jets from Logan cruised the black sky overhead. I could smell the first dew in the grass of the outfield, popcorn, hot dogs, spilled beer. "I've got to go," I said reluctantly. "If you hear anything you think I can use, let me know." Just then Ellis Burks hit a long drive into right field, and two Red Sox base runners scored. I stayed a few minutes longer, and when the hot dog vendor came our way I bought one, unwrapped it from the hot plastic wrap, and smeared it with yellow mustard. My beer was warm, but I drank it with the hot dog.

At the end of five innings the Sox were ahead five to zip, after Evans hit a homer over the wall with two men on. I wanted to stay, but I also wanted to make a few phone calls that night. So as Detroit came to bat in the sixth inning, I slipped out, leaving Baldo to eat and drink his way to the end.

CHAPTER FIFTEEN

Just Because
You're Paranoid . . .

IT WAS A SHORT WALK back to my apartment, through Kenmore Square where the bars were heating up, down Beacon to the little park at Charlesgate and my block. I thought there was a good chance Varega had caught up with Jack Eden, and he was dead. I wondered what kind of torture had been devised to compensate for three million stolen dollars—or if it was still going on, in a basement somewhere. There were aspects of Jack Eden's looniness that had been appealing, and I almost felt sorry for him.

But if he'd used Varega's money to fund the purchase of Eden's Garden, he'd left me with a legacy of trouble. I wondered if Blackstone and George Amory were trying to deal with the same legacy—if Eden had been partners with Blackstone, was Blackstone now partners with Varega? I was glad I had Mary in a safe place.

It was just after nine when I got upstairs. The phone in my bedroom was ringing. It was Dana McOscar.

"Have you eaten?" she said.

"A hot dog at the ball park."

"How about one of those Indian restaurants in Cambridge?"

"Sure. Pick you up in fifteen minutes."

I was thinking about Dana, trying to decide what to do about her and her brother, as I walked out to the Rambler and spotted a black Chrysler sedan double-parked at the end of the block by Charlesgate. When I pulled off Marlborough Street and swung around the corner to the Storrow Drive entrance, the Chrysler was a hundred yards behind me, keeping pace.

Once on the drive, I dropped my speed to forty. The other traffic whizzed by, but the black Chrysler hung back. There were silhouettes of two men in the front seat.

It looked as if I'd provoked a reaction from somebody. If the men in the Chrysler had been sent by Harvey Blackstone, they'd be professionals. The mainstream of traffic swung out to pass them, then accelerated on beyond me. That left a hundred yards of empty highway separating the Rambler from the Chrysler. The emptiness of that gap was ominous.

I accelerated, hitting one of the S-curves at the end of the drive in a manner to which the Rambler was not born. The traffic closed in behind me. I hoped for luck at the lights where the O'Brien Highway intersects with Storrow and all the traffic gets channeled up the ramp to the expressway. I got the luck. The Rambler was the last car through the red light before a wall of cross traffic jammed the intersection.

I looked in the rearview mirror and saw the black Chrysler three cars back into the line at the light. It suddenly swung right, over the curb and onto the grass, took down one of the big plywood signs for Charles River Apartments—IF YOU LIVED HERE YOU'D BE HOME BY NOW—and plowed aggressively through the intersection and up the ramp. Damned Boston drivers, I thought.

At the top of the ramp three major arteries intersect in an impossible junction. I stayed left, for Route 93, and at the last second cut off a beige Subaru to power my way onto the exit for 95 and the Mystic Tobin Bridge. The Chrysler rammed the Subaru, taking it sideways into the exit, then broke free from the lock of bumpers and followed.

We raced down the hill toward the bridge. The exit for

Charlestown had been closed as part of the renovation of the old shipyard. I thought, What the hell, and crashed through the wooden barricade. It felt like the long swoop off the high point of a roller coaster. I shot between cement mixers and stacks of wire rods looming on each side. Then I came to a full stop on the quiet stretch of Henley Street where it runs under the highway. Nobody followed.

Dana buzzed me in. There wasn't any elevator, and I walked to the fourth floor before I found her, standing at the open door of her apartment. She wore blue jeans and a faded green T-shirt, and she was barefoot. She said, "Come in. I'm not quite ready."

She told me there was wine in the kitchen, then disappeared through a door into what was obviously the bedroom. I went to stand at the bay windows in front, automatically scanning the street below for prowling black Chryslers.

In one of those odd flashes of memory, I recalled looking down on dark streets from another high window in a very different part of the world—Lima, Peru—at a time when soldiers armed with submachine guns patrolled the neighborhoods after curfew. I remembered thinking at the time that it'd be a great spot from which to watch the start of a revolution. The streets of Charlestown had the same brooding feel of potential violence that night.

Dana stepped up behind me, carrying two glasses of red wine, and handed one to me. "This view's one reason I live here," she said. Then it occurred to her I hadn't been looking at the view, and she said, "You don't have to worry about George. He's out of town tonight."

"It's not that. Somebody followed me here, or at least tried to. I lost them getting off the Charlestown exit from Route 95."

"That exit's closed."

"Exactly," I said, and took a drink of the wine.

She gave me a funny look, then said, "So who were they?"

"Could have been the people after my eccentric lady with the trust fund." Then I remembered Harold Peters's parting shot in Mangenello's office—"We'll be watching you"—and I smiled. "Could even have been the FBI," I said.

"Why the FBI?"

I sat on the couch that was set in the bay of the windows, and Dana joined me. "Because of another lawyer friend. One of the bad ones, at least according to the lawyer's code."

"What'd he do?"

"Stole six million dollars from a client, wire-transferred their money to his own account in the Bahamas." I laughed. "I guess he was a bad one by anybody's code, not just the ABA's. The FBI's still looking for Frank. They thought I was his accomplice, and they keep waiting for me to spend big chunks of money."

"You're like me. You don't really like lawyers, but you surround yourself with them."

I smiled at the thought that Dana had forgotten she herself was a lawyer. She'd have a lot of fun when her new job started. "I have a cynical appreciation for their way of looking at reality," I said. "When I started law school, I thought the lawyer's code of ethics had something to do with morality, and I figured lawyers had been thinking about that subject for years, so they might have some insights for me. Then I found out the primary concern of the code was something called 'the appearance of impropriety.' "

I stopped talking, but Dana sat waiting, smiling slightly.

"Your Judge Chapman gave his students an example of a code violation he particularly enjoyed," I went on. " 'A lawyer takes ten thousand dollars from a client's funds and invests them in the stock market. Two weeks later the lawyer has doubled his investment, and returns the original funds to the account, with a generous interest payment. The client never finds out. What's wrong with what the lawyer did?' "

She nodded, and I said, "At first I thought Chapman was being cynical when he told that story, but the more I thought it out, the more I realized he was being an idealist, because he thought the lawyer was wrong despite the appearance of propriety. Of course, in the real world, the lawyer would get away scot-free."

"You're wrong," Dana said. "The Judge told me that story too. He also told me why he stopped using it as an example for young lawyers. One of his students acted out the hypothetical after graduation."

I raised an eyebrow. "But he got caught?"

"That's right. Turned out to be somebody I knew, somebody from Amory and Harcourt. Poor John Prescott stole from the rich, made it rich, and then put the seed money back in the client's account. But he couldn't resist talking about it afterward. He told some associate who immediately went to Bill Amory and turned him in. The Judge was sitting in single-justice session when the disbarment proceedings came before the court."

"What'd he do?"

"Disbarred him, of course."

"Paradise lost."

"What?"

"It's how Frank described the process of disbarment. Satan cast down from heaven. Frank was disbarred himself, of course. *In absentia.*"

"He sounds like quite a character. I'll show you the Judge's opinion regarding John Prescott sometime, it's quite eloquent."

She stopped talking and we both turned and looked over the

back of the couch, out to the city lights and the skyline. "Do you really want to go out?" she said at last. "I have a can of Spaghettios I could heat up, and the rest of a bottle of Chianti."

I was tempted, but it somehow didn't seem the right thing to do. She was young, and there was George, and Mary was probably right, I like to avoid emotional complications. So I said, "Let's try for the Indian food. I haven't had any since the last time I was in Pittsburgh."

"Pittsburgh?"

"It's a long story." I told it on the way down the stairs and out to the Rambler. I drove us down the hill and away from the monument onto Main Street, headed for Cambridge. Dana stayed quiet on her side of the front seat, absently watching the buildings at the side of the road. It was not an uncomfortable silence. As we turned off Main Street onto Charlestown Avenue, I looked in the rearview mirror and spotted the black Chrysler.

Either they'd been cruising the neighborhood and got incredibly lucky, or they'd known where I was going and waited for me somewhere off Monument Square. I told Dana we were being followed.

"What do they want?"

"If it's the FBI, probably just to follow. If it's somebody else, there might be trouble."

We went under the high concrete supports that suspend Route 93 over Charlestown Community College, then started over the empty wasted area where the canal cuts in from the Charles River. The Charlestown Prison once squatted in the mists of that canal—it's where Sacco and Vanzetti got iced by the state. The road was four lanes wide, without a median strip, and there was no other traffic. The Chrysler moved into the left lane and closed on us, then pulled alongside.

The face of the man in the passenger's seat was covered by a black ski mask. He was holding a gun. I slammed on the brakes, heard the sharp *ping* of the high-velocity bullet hitting the hood of the Rambler. When we were stopped with the Rambler slewed sideways across the roadway, I threw it into reverse and accelerated into a spin turn, then shot back in the direction of Charlestown.

The Chrysler didn't follow. I understood why when I saw the cop car coming along behind us. Dana sat up in the seat beside me, her face gone very pale, but when she saw me watching her she managed a smile and a short exhalation of breath. "Wow."

I slowed so the cop car passed. If he'd seen any of the reckless driving a moment earlier, it didn't seem to interest him. I pulled into the small shopping center at the corner of Main Street and stopped.

"I should have figured they might be back," I said. "I shouldn't have taken you with me."

Dana didn't answer, just took off her seat belt, moved close, and put her arms around me. I could feel the warmth of her through the T-shirt and her moist, shallow breathing against my neck. After a long moment she said into my ear, "I got their license plate number."

I held her back away from me and said, "You're kidding."

"Eighty-five thirty-five U," she said.

Five minutes later I sat on Dana's couch, talking on the phone with Mangenello. Dana had left the room. I gave Simon the license plate number.

"It was probably stolen, and they've probably ditched it by now," I said, "but it's worth a shot."

"Okay, I'll get on it." And he hung up. I put down the phone. Dana walked back into the room, wearing a black terry-cloth robe. She came over to kneel in front of me.

"This probably isn't a good idea," I said.

She smiled and shook her head no, then pulled off the robe. She was all pale-pink skin underneath, her breasts pushed against my knees as she put her arms out to be held.

"Okay," I said, and my voice had suddenly gotten very hoarse. "You've convinced me."

I never did get a proper supper that night.

CHAPTER SIXTEEN

Only the Good . . .

"WE GOT LUCKY," Simon said.

It was ten o'clock the next morning and I sat in his office at 1010 Commonwealth Avenue, along with Joe Mariosa, the DEA agent, holding a mug shot. It showed both the face and profile of a young Latino with a thin nose, sunken cheeks, and skin scarred with acne. His eyes were turned slightly from the camera, but nevertheless managed to convey both indifference and menace. The photograph said he was number PX10034, also known as Marcos Solano.

"We got lucky," Simon said again. "The Chrysler was stolen off St. Botolphe late yesterday afternoon—the owner reported it when he got home from work. I pulled some strings with Boston P.D. and they sent men out to knock on doors. It was a long shot, but they came up with a woman who'd witnessed the theft from her apartment window."

"Why didn't she report it?" Mariosa said.

"Happened so quick, she figured the guy had keys to the car. But she remembered him. Looked through two books of mug shots and picked him out, positive ID."

"Is he freelance or connected?" I said.

"Freelance, far as I can tell. He's got three priors for grand theft auto, one for assault. At the moment he's waiting trial for driving getaway on a botched bank job."

"Where is he now?"

"We're looking for him. He's got a room in a firetrap on Dudley Street but hasn't been home. The firetrap belongs to your pal Harvey Blackstone. It's an interesting coincidence."

"Except Blackstone owns half the city," I said. "Can I keep this picture?"

"Sure. I've got a man watching Solano's room, but I don't know how much longer I can keep him there."

"What about DEA agents?" I said to Mariosa.

"I've been cut off," he said, frowning. "The brass doesn't want to spend any more time on Eden. I'm officially on leave of absence without pay." And he added grimly, "For as long as it takes."

"I'm not officially in on this either," Simon said. "The Commonwealth hasn't opened a file on Eden Development. Nevertheless, I got a question. If we manage to pick up Solano, is it going to help us any?"

"We want to find the person or persons behind Eden Development," I said. "If Solano works for them, he's got to have a point of contact. We find him, put a tail on him, and wait for the next contact."

"Except that after last night," Simon answered me, "Solano's probably on the run. There isn't going to be any more contact."

"So we pull him in and squeeze the information out of him," Mariosa said.

"It's a long shot," I added. "But it's the only wedge they've left us so far."

"Let's hope Varega or Eden or one of Blackstone's pals hasn't taken care of Solano, then. We got an all–New England bulletin out on the little putz. You got any other ideas how to bring him in any quicker?"

"I'll work on it," I said.

* * *

I went from headquarters at Commonwealth Avenue to the Trojan and dialed Barbi's number in Weston. Mary answered on the seventh ring, and when I asked how she was feeling she said, "I have nightmares every time I close my eyes, and I miss my cats. But your friend has been very kind."

"I'm calling because there's been a breakthrough in the case." I told her about Jack Eden and Varega.

She let me go on for a few minutes, then interrupted. "So why aren't you looking for them?"

"Because my next step will be to spend a chunk of your money to find a man who could lead me to Eden or Varega. Before I do that, I thought you should know the police might do the same job for you, free of charge."

"If I'd wanted the police I'd have called them. You know how I feel about that. You go ahead, spend what you need. I can afford it. If something happens to me, you keep after them. I've made arrangements for you to be paid."

"Nothing's going to happen to you, Mary. As long as you stay put."

"I'm tired of staying put," she said. There was silence on the line for half a minute. Then she said, "Don't worry, Mallory, I'll stay put. I wouldn't go anyplace without my cats."

After I'd hung up I went to the floor safe, took out ten hundred-dollar bills and five twenties. I grabbed the photos of Solano, Varega, and Eden, locked the office, and went down the back stairs to the alley where I park the Rambler.

Mariosa sat in a blue Plymouth four-door sedan, parked against the back wall of the old Bradford Hotel. I went over and stood beside the car.

"I want to come along on this jaunt," he said.

"Then you take orders from me," I told him.

"Get in," he said. "We'll use my car."

I got in. As we drove out of the alley he said, "Where to, boss?"

On Brookline Street, just off Harrison Avenue in the South End, there's a beer joint that sells pizza and subs. It's owned by a Greek named Johnnie Avalahoutas, and it gets a mixed crowd— mostly nurses and doctors tired of the cafeteria food at nearby University Hospital, and unemployed kids from the neighbor- hood who come to play the pinball machines. On the outside it looks like it's been boarded up after a fire, but inside it's clean and well lighted, with red vinyl booths lining one wall and a long counter running the length of the other, pizza ovens and beer on tap behind the counter.

I told Mariosa to wait for me in the car and went in. Mal- colm Fox sat in a booth at the far end of the room, drinking beer. I ordered a Budweiser and took it down to sit opposite him.

"Hello, Mallory," he said. "What you want?"

Malcolm is one of those free agents who operate on the fringes of the law, sometimes as a pimp or gun dealer, sometimes as a thug employment agency, and when money is low, as a po- lice snitch. I'd met him in the latter capacity while sitting in on a murder investigation with my old friend Cromerty of the Boston detective bureau. When I later went to Malcolm for information on another case, he got it for me "on the house." Since then I'd been a steady, paying customer. It's been three years, and each time I see Malcolm still alive and sitting in his booth I marvel at his capacity for survival. Maybe he's just too useful to be killed.

I took out the picture of Solano and said, "You know him?"

He took a quick look and said, "It's my business to know

men like Solano," then he grinned. "I give you the name gratis since what you got there is a police photo."

"Know where he is?"

"I can find out. When you need him?"

"Now."

"Gonna cost you. What you want him for?"

"Does it matter?"

"Okay. Give me half an hour."

Once out of the booth Malcolm stood only five feet above the floor—his legs are too short for his torso. We shook hands, and when the shake ended he had five of Mary's hundred-dollar bills in his palm.

I sat in the bar and had another beer and a cheeseburger sub while I waited. It was forty-five minutes before Malcolm returned, but when he did he looked pleased with himself.

He said, "My sources place him at a rooming house on Tremont Street," and he gave me the number. "Seems a friend of his lets him crash there. The friend is out of town. You still not packing a gun?"

"Right."

"I can get you one, nice police special. This dude's armed and dangerous."

"I'll manage."

"That why you got the Spanish guy waitin' in the car for you? He your guardian angel? He looks like a cop to me, but then, you always did like cops."

I didn't say anything, but pulled out the pictures of Eden and Varega. "You seen either of these guys around? They're from Miami. Cocaine."

"Just say no, man. I ain't seen them. But I'll let you know if I do."

"Thanks, Malcolm."

*   *   *

When I got back to the Plymouth Mariosa was drinking coffee from a Styrofoam cup and reading the *Globe*. "Got him," I said. "Tremont Street."

He dumped the cup out the window, gunned the engine, and spun out onto Brookline.

"I feel like I've been real useful to you," he said.

"Next time you can come in with me. Solano's got a gun."

"Thanks." We cruised past the little park at Franklin Square. "You think he might really lead us to Eden?"

"To Eden or Varega or Harvey Blackstone. Take your pick—though I have a feeling Eden's dead."

"No way. I've been chasing the guy too long. I'd know if he was dead." It was a flat statement of fact.

"More instinct?" I said.

He looked embarrassed. "I expect that from someone like Peters, but not you. How long you been a PI?"

"Thirteen years."

"Then you should know about instinct. Like when you're looking for a guy, you get the feeling about a certain bar, sure enough, he's in there drinking. You're in the right place at the right time. Maybe it's just luck, like hitting the right number in roulette—but don't tell me it's never happened to you. I know Eden's not dead."

"Why are you doing this, Mariosa? Why don't you go home to your wife and kids and get on with your job?"

"Because when I do, I want to be able to hold my head up high."

He spun us out onto Tremont Street where it cuts, wide and straight, through a beat-up neighborhood of old tenements and boarded-up storefronts. The rooming house was a big granite structure with an elaborate but decaying stone entrance. Mariosa double-parked on the street and we went in. The outsized marble lobby was empty except for a small metal desk with a phone, and at the desk an attendant, a black man in his sixties. He looked up from a copy of *Penthouse* and asked what we wanted.

Mariosa pulled out his badge. "We want to talk with one of your tenants. Marcos Solano."

"He don't live here."

"Room 412," I said.

"I don't know nothin' about that."

"Better come with us," Mariosa told him. We used the elevator. It was slow, dimly lighted, and smelled like piss. The fourth-floor corridor smelled like piss too. I told the old man to wait by the elevator, and he mumbled some complaint under his breath.

Outside room 412, I stood beside the door and listened. A radio was playing inside. Mariosa had his gun out. I heard the elevator start—the attendant was retreating. I stepped away from the wall, gave the door a hard, short kick just below the latch. It popped open and Mariosa went in.

I waited for the sound of a gun, or Mariosa's voice, or something. There was nothing but the radio. I looked in and saw an unmade single bed, a yellow shag carpet, a big stereo speaker at the foot of the bed. A man's legs were stretched out on the floor. They belonged to Marcos Solano.

Mariosa stood over him, the fingers of his left hand clenching and unclenching. "Son of a bitch," he said. I stooped and felt at the artery in Solano's neck, then pulled his shirt open and found where the knife blade had gone in, between the ribs and up into the heart. The body was still warm. Even over the sour smell of death, I caught a whiff of his rancid sweat.

Mariosa said, "I'll call from downstairs," and left.

I looked down at the thin, pockmarked face of the dead man. The eyes were open. They were no longer menacing or indifferent. The radio played a Billy Joel song. I spent the next fifteen minutes looking carefully through the room for anything that might lead us to his killer, but found nothing.

CHAPTER SEVENTEEN

Champerty in Sangerville

IT OCCURRED TO ME that whoever had killed Solano—and my instincts told me it was Varega—might decide at that point to cut his losses and run. I wasn't sure what that would mean for Mary, or for the future of Eden's Garden, but I hoped he hadn't. He'd hired someone to beat up my client, he'd shot at me and Dana, and now he'd casually murdered a man I was looking for. I wanted the chance to retaliate.

If there was a weak link in the chain of circumstances leading to the creation of Eden Development, it had to be George Amory. If I could find out how Eden had made contact with George, that might give me a starting point to find Eden. If George was still in contact, if he was part of the conspiracy or whatever it was, then so much the better.

I could probably have got to him through Dana, but I vetoed that. I'd had dinner at her place earlier that evening, after spending most of the afternoon at the Berkeley Street police station in the company of homicide detectives. Over dinner I'd told her about Eden Development, Jack Eden, and Varega. We'd avoided discussing George Amory, although I was sure we'd both been thinking about him. Some of my thoughts had to do with his relationship to Dana—I wasn't sure where she stood with him, and I knew she was trying to work that out—and some had to do with the logistics of breaking into his office to get to the files on Eden Development.

I left Dana's at ten, forgetting my jacket, which still had the photos of Eden, Varega, and Solano, plus six hundred dollars in cash, stuffed in the pockets. Freud would interpret my forgetting the jacket as a sign that I hadn't wanted to leave, and he'd be right.

Michael met me at the Parker House bar, where four nights earlier we'd discussed the problem of tracking down the principals of Eden Development. Since Michael's firm was in the same building as Amory & Harcourt, I planned to use him as an accessory.

He wasn't happy about it. We left the bar, drove to the building in his Mercedes, and parked in his place in the underground garage. He got us past the two security guards in the lobby, signing his name on the sheet and putting a check mark in the space for "guest." As we rode up in the elevator he said, "I hope I won't regret this."

"If anything happens, you tell them I was here to talk about the case. When I left I snuck down to A and H without your knowledge or consent."

"Certainly without my approval. Just remember, the security guards patrol the building at irregular intervals, and it's possible there'll be people working down there. How will I know if something happens to you?"

"If I'm not back thirty minutes after I head down there, call George's private line. If I don't answer, assume the worst."

We got off the elevator on the thirty-sixth floor, and I sat in Michael's office and drank a beer before going to work. He had a big corner room looking out to the harbor and the lights of East Boston. You could see lit-up cruise boats pulling away from Rowes Wharf and the occasional small plane coming in to land at Logan. When enough time had elapsed to justify the story that we were talking business, I got up without saying anything and went out to the reception area. From a bookcase crammed with learned treatises, I chose a volume marked *Lewdness to Liens,* and used it to prop open the door to the fire exit. Then I took the cement and steel staircase down six flights, to Bill Amory's floor.

Two days earlier I'd noticed the wide double doors leading in from the elevators were secured by electronic combination locks, which can be a problem. They hadn't been as careful with the fire doors, and in less than a minute the standard lock snapped open and I stood inside, taking a moment to orient myself, listening for the sound of anyone still on the premises cranking out a complaint or a memorandum of law. I didn't expect company that late on a Friday night. The corridor was dimly lit, the offices along its length were dark, except for the shadowy glow from the windows.

Dana had told me George's office was next door to his father's. I found his nameplate on the Cambridge side of the building and switched on the overhead fluorescents. People on the street would see the lit-up cubicle high on the side of the building, and those in the know would figure it was another young associate burning the midnight oil. The office was small, but furnished with an expensive walnut desk and matching cabinets. There was little to indicate George had invested any of his personality in the room—except on the desk, a head-and-shoulders snapshot of Dana, in a green porcelain frame.

I checked the Rolodex, but there wasn't a listing for Eden Development. In the desk drawers I came across a computer printout of telephone calls dating back over a year, pulled the sheets for April and May, folded them twice, and put them in my back pocket. There was nothing else in the desk of any interest, and I moved over to a file cabinet across the room.

I got lucky and found a file labeled EDEN DEVELOPMENT— REAL ESTATE PURCHASE. It was a very thin file, copies of deeds and a few letters to and from counsel for the original owner, Anthony D'Amato. A memo to the file stated that Eden had been informed of its duties with respect to payment of income taxes on any resale of the property and that Eden had assured counsel that funds for the purchase price were derived from legitimate sources. I was willing to bet the memo was of recent vintage—it might as well have been captioned "Re: Covering Our Ass."

The correspondence was in chronological order, two-hole-punched and clipped to the file, and I almost missed a pink message slip at the very beginning of the chronology. Perhaps someone purging the file of incriminating evidence had also missed it. It was dated April 25. In the space for "message from" the name "Mr. Prescott" had been scrawled in blue ink, and the box for "will call back" had been checked. There wasn't any phone number for Prescott.

I put the file back in its drawer and returned to the desk. The phone had ten buttons for speed dialing, nine of them labeled. I picked up the receiver and punched the button without a label. After the clicks of the dialing mechanism and two short rings a recorded voice answered and told me I'd reached the offices of Harvey Blackstone.

I was speculating on the significance of that when George Amory stepped into the room, pointed a gun at my face, and said, "Hang up."

It was an antique dueling pistol held in a white-knuckled hand, with the hammer pulled back—so any tightening of the finger on the hair trigger would deal me a very sudden, theatrical, and messy death. I put down the receiver, said, "You don't want to shoot me, George."

"Don't count on it!" he shouted, and shook the pistol at me. "What are you doing here? Why do you keep messing up my life?"

"It's Eden Development, not me, George." I glanced at the clock on the wall over the file cabinet.

"What the hell's going on between you and Dana?"

"Dana has nothing to do with this. You're in trouble, George. I can help. Tell me who Prescott is. How's he connected to Eden Development?" Then I remembered; Prescott was the name of the lawyer Dana had told me about, the one who'd stolen from his client and been disbarred.

George saw the expression on my face and said, too quickly, "You're crazy, he doesn't have anything to do with Eden."

"Where is he now?"

"I don't know what you're talking about."

"Rich young lawyers don't go to jail, George, not if they're smart. Talk to me. How's Blackstone connected to Eden?"

He shook his head, lowered the gun a notch, and took a few deep breaths. "I don't know what you're talking about. I'm going to call security."

He kept his eyes focused on me, and I glanced again at the clock. The timing couldn't have been better. George reached for the phone, and as his hand tightened on the receiver—it rang. He jerked back like he'd been bitten. I took two quick steps to close with him, grabbed the gun. He resisted, and in a sudden excess of vexation, I drove my fist up into his solar plexus—one quick, hard blow that loosened his grip on the pistol and sent him back into the swivel chair with a *woof!*

I held the gun at my side, picked up the phone, said, "Thank you for being punctual. Fifteen more minutes," heard Michael's voice say "Right," and hung up.

Bill Amory hadn't lied about his guns—the pistol was primed and ready to kill. I pointed it at George. "You hurt me," he said, his face darkening as he held both hands to his middle.

I looked at him for a full minute, then said, "I'm sorry, but now we're going to talk."

He shook his head. "I can't."

I put the pistol up against his forehead. He shied away from it but said through clenched teeth, "You're not going to shoot me."

I lowered the gun.

"I can't tell you anything," he said. "They're my clients." His face came apart as he started to cry. I removed the firing cap, left the pistol on the desk beside the photo of Dana, and went.

Michael got us two cold Heinekens and sat down to look through the printout of phone calls. "Looks like the same system we have," he said. "The computer keeps track of every outgoing call on each phone in the office for billing purposes. Unfortunately, it doesn't record the originating number on incoming calls. Unless George called this Prescott guy back, these sheets won't give us his number." He put his finger on the thin paper and began to scan the page. "Here's one he called three times that day."

"Look up Blackstone's number, see if it's the same."

Instead he pushed a button to turn on his conference speakers and punched out the number. There was a click, then the message on Harvey's machine began to broadcast over the speakers. Michael cocked an eyebrow at me and switched off the machine. "Of course," he said, "George could have had other business with Blackstone."

"What do you know about this guy Prescott?"

"I remember when he was disbarred, but not many details." He looked at his watch and said, "Judy's gonna be pissed if I try to tell her I was working at the office past midnight."

"Dana mentioned an opinion the Judge had written. Would that be in the casebooks?"

"Sure. A disbarment proceeding is public information. Let's take a look."

We went down to the firm's library. It had a royal-blue carpet, solid teak bookcases, and the same view of Cambridge

George Amory had from his office. Michael used the index and found "*In re* John Prescott."

He paged through the opinion. "Doesn't say much. A lot of rhetoric about the appearance of impropriety and the public trust placed in attorneys. Prescott borrowed a hundred thousand from his client's account, invested it in the stock market. He doubled the hundred grand, reimbursed the client account, and kept the profits."

"Who was the client?"

"Doesn't say. To the extent they can, they like to keep these things confidential." He closed the book with a snap and put it back on the shelf. "What now?"

"See if you can find out where Prescott ended up."

"I'll work on it. Think we're getting any closer to Eden Development?"

"I think we're almost there."

It was close to one in the morning when I got home, but I called Dana anyway to ask if she wanted late-night company. I woke her. She kept her voice low and told me too formally that it wouldn't be a good idea. From the way she spoke I knew she wasn't alone, and that made my stomach go hollow. I could guess what had happened. I'd humiliated George, and he'd gone to seek comfort. I told Dana to sleep well and hung up.

I called Della to check my messages. There was one from Jay saying he'd hit on something important while running his title search of Ben's property. I called and he answered on the first ring.

"Been sitting here at my desk, too restless to sleep," he said. "I took your advice and ran Ben's name through the index at the registry. That woodlot Clive Linscott told you he owned? He sold it to Ben twenty-five years ago."

"Sold it? Judge Chapman said the title was litigated and Clive lost. You sure the deed wasn't part of the settlement?"

"I doubt it. If it was a settlement, Linscott would have given Ben a quit-claim deed, not one with full warranties. Besides, there's nothing in the chain of title giving Ben any claim."

"Does the deed show a purchase price?"

"No—doesn't have to in Maine. There's something else, Jimmy. I found at least twenty quit-claim deeds running to Ben, all recorded in the last two years. Different properties all over town. All of the deeds were from people out of the chain of title. You know what champerty is?"

"Ben was snatching land from his neighbors?"

"That's right. And something really odd. For the past six months he had a partner. Remember the guy I mentioned who bought the land at the end of Ben's road? Jack Eden."

I felt the rush of blood to my heart, the same feeling I'd once had in Vegas, when I'd plunked a fifty-dollar chip on number 22 and saw it turn up on the wheel. I said, "You never mentioned his name."

"No? Starting five months ago, about the time he first showed up in town, Eden's on the deeds as a grantee along with Ben. They're joint tenants. That means all the rights went to Eden when Ben died."

"You handled Eden's closing," I said. "Did he give you an address or telephone number?"

"Let me check the file."

A minute later his voice came back. "I remember now, he was touchy about giving an address. All I have is a private post office box, in Boston."

"Box 331," I said.

There was silence on the line. "You already knew the address? How about the telephone number?"

The words lifted my spirits. "Give it to me."

"It's down in Massachusetts somewhere, 617–555-8967. What the hell's going on, Jimmy?"

"I'm not sure yet. Have you seen Eden recently?"

"Not for months. There's one other thing. According to the clerk at the registry, Judge Chapman did a search of Ben's properties early this week. He must know about those funny deeds."

"So why hasn't he told anyone? I think he's trying to protect the Chapman family name. Do me a favor, Jay. Don't try to contact Eden, and don't tell anyone about those quit-claim deeds. I'll be in Sangerville tomorrow or Sunday."

"Joint ownership of those deeds gave Eden a motive to kill Ben, you know. Maybe I should tell McGuire."

"Not anyone, especially not McGuire. Trust me. We'll talk about it when I get up there."

After we'd hung up, I called the operator. She told me the number Jay'd given me was in the Truro exchange, a small town close to Provincetown on the tip of Cape Cod. But when I called information, they told me there weren't any Jack Edens in Truro. If the number was unlisted, a friend at the phone company could check it for me and pull the address. For that I'd have to wait until Monday. If I called the number and Eden was there, it might spook him.

I had a hunch. I called information again and asked for John Prescott of Truro. The operator said, "I have a Jack Prescott on Cooper Road."

"I'll try it," I said. The computerized voice kicked in. "The number is . . . 555 . . . 8967." The same number Jay had given me. And I thought, Jack Prescott was disbarred three months before Jack Eden showed up at Miami International Airport, smuggling his first batch of cocaine through customs. Eden's telephone number on the Cape was listed under Prescott's name. Prescott was Eden.

CHAPTER EIGHTEEN

Cape Cod

EARLY THE NEXT MORNING I thawed three croissants and made a pot of coffee for the Thermos, then took my picnic breakfast down to the Rambler. The air smelled clean and salty, with a fresh breeze from the ocean, and I looked forward to the long drive south to the Cape. There was no traffic on Storrow Drive or the expressway, and in twenty minutes I was beyond downtown, with City Hospital on my right and South Boston off in the distance on my left. When I passed the Dorchester oil tanks I poured the Thermos cap full of coffee and had my first croissant.

People have been driving from Boston to Cape Cod since cars were invented, and parts of the road are so old they have unnecessary curves built into them, to make the journey more aesthetically pleasing. Closer to the Cape, the highway narrows and crosses a long flat of shrub pines in sand. Then come the bridges, giant steel arches spanning the wide shipping canal built by the Army Corps of Engineers. The only way to get on or off the Cape—except by boat or plane—is to cross one of the two bridges, and on a Friday night in summer they create the biggest traffic bottleneck on the eastern seaboard.

As I drove, sipping my coffee and savoring the croissants, I started to formulate a theory that would explain the creation of Eden Development, the advent of violence at Eden's Garden, and the apparently inexplicable connection of Jack Eden to Sangerville, Maine. It all looked like another elaborate Jack Eden practical joke, this time a deadly one, with the same motive that had inspired the nasty surprises he'd left behind for his enemies in Miami: revenge. In this case, revenge against everyone who'd participated in his public censure and disbarment.

By putting Varega's money into Boston real estate, Eden had left behind a legacy of trouble. But the legacy wasn't inadvertent, as I'd first thought. If Eden left Varega enough clues to track down his stolen money, then Varega's arrival in Boston was inevitable. I wasn't sure how the disgruntled partner fit into things now—but he was clearly a monkey wrench in somebody's works.

And Ben Chapman? His death could have been Judge Chapman's punishment for presiding over the disbarment proceedings. Why or how Hank had been framed for the murder was something I couldn't yet explain. One thing was clear: like Mariosa's person in the right place at the right time, I'd somehow come up in the middle of things.

I was also willing to bet Mariosa had been right about Eden—that he was still alive, sitting it out somewhere, watching the chips fall into place. I was hoping "somewhere" would be Truro. Finding him wouldn't unravel the mess he'd created, but I'd start with the basics and deal with the mess later.

Truro is ten miles south of Provincetown, on the bay side of the long hook that makes the Cape. I almost missed the turn-off for Cooper Road—it was narrow and closed in by brush. The surface had been tarred at some time in the distant past, but the only evidence of that fact were scattered slabs of macadam undercut by potholes. It was the type of road only the rich can afford to maintain—it assures them a modicum of privacy and presents no serious problem to the suspension systems designed for them by German automakers. The Rambler was designed for cruising down the broad thoroughfares of Detroit, and it did a lot of bouncing.

I negotiated a steep decline and came into an area of old dunes that had grown over with wild roses and cranberry bushes. I couldn't see the bay yet, but I could tell where it must be, over a ridge up ahead that had a lot of emptiness behind it. The little valley was dotted with big vacation homes, all of them plunked down in that wasteland of sand and brush for only one reason— the wide water on the other side of the ridge.

Prescott's house had a prime location, on the crest facing out to the bay. It was a modern A-frame, with a two-car garage on the lower level. The place had a whimsical name, burned into a pine signboard hung from the rural mailbox: PRESCOTT FARM. The name was whimsical because no beans or squash or corn would ever grow in that sandy soil, nourished by brackish water.

I parked in a turn-off and found a trail running up the side of the ridge, between a double hedge of wild roses that bordered Prescott Farm. From the top of the ridge I could see the slender campanile of the watchtower rising above Provincetown, five miles across the bay. A hundred feet below, down a slope of loose white sand, a few hundred near-naked people were stretched out on beach blankets, reading novels by Tama Janowitz and Judith Krantz.

On the sea side the A-frame was all glass, opening onto a cedar deck that projected several feet out over the edge of the precipice. I left the trail and crossed the intervening twenty yards of brush, keeping low enough so anyone inside wouldn't spot me, then peered over the platform of the deck to look through the front window. There were two people in the room, a woman and man, making love on the floor. The woman was on top, facing away from me.

I waited for them to finish, doing my best to maintain a professional detachment. It didn't take long, and they didn't exchange any caresses or other endearments when it was over, or even stop to savor the view out the picture window. They moved to a couch and started cutting lines from a substantial pile of white powder on the glass top of a coffee table. They both had short blond hair and flushed faces. The man wasn't Jack Eden. I climbed up onto the deck and walked in through the open slider. I said, "Don't move, I'm a cop."

The guy started to stand, and I made a little jerking motion with my hand in my pocket. It was corny, but it worked. It probably helped that I was bigger than him and fully clothed, and he was naked. I said, "Where's Prescott?"

The guy looked relieved by the question. "I don't know. Jack lets me use this place. This isn't even my cocaine."

"A seagull dropped it through the skylight, right?"

He laughed nervously and put down the razor blade. I rummaged through a heap of clothing on a chair by the window, found a wallet and purse. In among the gold cards in the wallet were ten crisp twenty-dollar bills, fresh from the money machine. His business card said he was Robert Jaffney, attorney-at-law at the firm of Amory & Harcourt. In the purse I found another business card—Penelope Hott, Esq., with the name and address of a different Boston law firm. I pocketed the cards.

"Where's Prescott?" I said again.

"I haven't seen him in months, honest," Robert said. "Jack lets me use this place."

"We don't have to tell him anything," Penelope said. She had a nice body and intelligent eyes. I went to the coffee table and took a taste of the white powder.

"Anything you say can and will be used against you in a court of law," I said. "But if you cooperate, I may let you walk out of here."

"I'd tell you if I could," Robert said, "but I don't know. Jack travels a lot. To tell you the truth, I haven't seen him since he left the firm three years ago." He gave the nervous laugh again.

"Tell me about that."

"We don't have to tell him anything," Penelope said again. "I'd like to see your identification."

"There's no reason I can't tell him what he wants to know," Robert said quickly. "This used to be Jack's weekend place. Jack and I started at the firm together—I was his best friend."

Penelope asked if she could put her clothes on, and I nodded. I kept one eye on her—when she was dressed she sat in a chair in the corner by the window. I made her come back to the couch. Robert kept talking.

"Jack was a crackerjack lawyer, but he had too damned much imagination. You guys must know about this—he stole from a client."

"Who was the client?"

"Harvey Blackstone. Big real estate tycoon."

That, of course, I'd guessed. Varega was the monkey wrench Eden had thrown into the works, and Harvey owned a piece of the works. How he'd been manipulated into becoming Eden's partner was another question.

"Were you the one who turned Jack in, Robert?"

"Hell, no. That was George Amory, the senior partner's son. He'd do anything to score a point with his old man." He seemed to remember he was talking to a cop, and added, "Not that I approve of what Jack did, of course."

"Why would Prescott tell George he'd stolen the money?"

"That's the way Jack is. He can't let things sit. Also, it wasn't as if he'd really stolen the money—he'd borrowed it and made a killing on the stock exchange, then he repaid every cent, with interest. He just never asked Blackstone for permission. I don't think Bill Amory would have pressed it, if Blackstone hadn't insisted. And Blackstone wouldn't have insisted if it wasn't for the kicker Jack threw in."

"Which was?"

"Jack took some of the money he made and contributed it to a tenants' group engaged in litigation over one of Blackstone's properties. It was like he was needling the guy. Jack liked a good joke, but sometimes he went overboard."

No kidding, I thought. I said, "What happened to him after he got disbarred?"

"He disappeared. He kept this place, but only a few of us knew about it and we kept it a secret."

I pointed to the cocaine and said, "Where'd that come from?"

The guy looked at the pile as if he'd just seen it, then said, "I don't know."

I said, "Get up and get dressed. Is your car in the garage?"

"Yes."

"I want you out of here. I've got your names. We'll be back in touch."

He gave me an ingratiating smile. "We've got a few things in the bedroom to pack. If you don't mind?"

After he'd pulled on his tight white chinos and Ralph Lauren shirt, the three of us went together into the bedroom. Penelope hadn't said a word since she'd put on her clothes, but I had the feeling she didn't approve of Robert's talking and had washed her hands of the whole matter. They started pulling clothing out of the drawers and closets. I said, "That's a lot of stuff for a week-end visit."

"Actually, we spend a lot of time down here," Robert said. "Jack never shows up. I've even started taking in his mail." He laughed. "In fact, I've been paying his monthly phone and electric bills."

"We're squatters," Penelope said.

Robert laughed again. "Something like that. Or house sitters. I sometimes wonder if Jack's dead—but I guess not, if you guys are after him. What's he been up to, smuggling drugs? You don't need to tell me. Jack bought this place when we were just starting at A and H, and I've always wondered where he got the money. He had a real thing about property. When he was a kid he lived in the South End. When his mom got sick and they couldn't pay the rent, the landlord threw them out. His mom died after that, and Jack ended up in foster homes. Pretty sad story."

"Finish packing," I said. I looked around the room. On shelves of a bedside table there was a leather-bound edition of Thoreau's *Journals* and a catalog for the Burpee Seed Company. The catalog had bright pictures of all the tomatoes and cabbages you could grow with Burpee seeds. The order form at the back of the book had been torn out.

Robert saw me looking at the catalog and said, "Jack always said he wanted to go to the country and live off the land, like Thoreau. He was kidding himself. He couldn't settle down in the woods any more than I could. He's a wild man."

While he'd been talking, I'd walked over to the bureau and picked up a framed photograph. It was a picture of people sailing—Dana McOscar facing the camera, Jack Eden at the helm. I wondered if George Amory had taken the shot. I removed it from the frame and brought it over to Robert. I pointed at Eden and said, "Is that Prescott?"

He looked surprised. "Sure."

I hustled them out of there and down to their red Porsche in the garage. They squeezed half a dozen bags into the back. When Robert was in the driver's seat, Penelope hung back a moment and surprised me. She said, "You're no cop, I can tell. But call me. Any time." Then she got in the car and Robert backed it away too fast, got stuck in the sand beyond the driveway, gunned it, and they took off.

I searched Eden's house from top to bottom. There was nothing to suggest he'd been there at any recent time, and no clue as to where he might be at present. But going through Thoreau's

Journals, looking for anything that might be hidden between the pages, I read the title on the spine of the very last of the numbered, leather-bound volumes. In the identical gold-filled script of the others it said "Not Thoreau's *Journal.*" I opened it and the first thing I saw was a copy of Harvey Blackstone's 1984 IRS filing.

The rest of it was similar information. Along with copies of official forms there were careful tabulations of properties owned by Blackstone—some under fictitious names—the number of apartments in each building, and the rents collected for each apartment. I read enough to see that it all added up to evidence that Blackstone had reported much less income from rents than he'd actually collected in each of the years documented. Somebody had spent a lot of time and money doing the research, and I guessed Eden had had private detectives working on the problem. I also guessed the volume had been left there for me—or somebody like me—to find.

I could use the phone in the bedroom, call Mariosa, and get him down there with a team. But I had told Jay I'd be in Maine that weekend, and the federal agents would tie me up with questions. Especially if, now that DEA had officially backed off from the case, the FBI and Harold Peters got involved. And I wanted time to think about how to use the material in the leather-bound journal.

After one last look at the view out to Provincetown, I headed down the stairs to the garage. My hand was on the knob of the door leading out when I spotted the black Mercedes parked in the driveway.

CHAPTER NINETEEN

The Black Mercedes

ON MY WAY back up the stairs, I heard him in the front room. He must have gone up the outside steps and come in from the deck. I ducked through an open archway into the kitchen, set the leather-bound notebook on the counter, and braced myself against the wall just inside the archway. I heard the sweep of the double-hinged door from the front, his step in the hall, then he walked into the kitchen with a .357 Magnum in his gun hand.

It was Varega. The notebook caught his eye, he took a step toward it, and I uncoiled from the wall—got my right hand on the gun, flattened the palm of my left against his back, and slammed him against the frame of the arch. The gun went off with a sharp explosion and the sound of breaking glass. When he bounced off the frame I clamped my left arm around his neck and spun him into the hallway. He was strong, but I had the advantage of height and surprise. I levered against the wall and sent us catapulting toward the door to the front room. His head crashed against the wood as the door popped open, then I lost my grip on his throat and went down on one knee. He surged through, tried to recover his footing, ran into the coffee table and went down in a cloud of cocaine dust.

I grabbed the gun he'd dropped and leveled it at his face.

The look he gave me made me glad to have the gun—it was an animal fury, the black eyes flashed, and for a second I thought he would charge me anyway. He was stocky and barrel-chested, with big, flat hands. Twice the width of the powerful wrists, they ended in short, swollen fingers. He opened his mouth in a wide contemptuous grimace and told me in Spanish to fuck my mother.

"Speak English," I said.

"Put away that fucking gun," he answered me, wiped coke dust and blood from his face with one of the big hands, then started to get up.

"Don't move," I said, and cocked the gun for emphasis. I wasn't going to take any chances with this one. He leaned back with his palms on the floor, gave me another evil look.

"What are you doing here?" I said.

He didn't answer. I said, "Looking for Jack Eden? Or is Eden dead?"

"You're dead."

I took a step forward, kicked the coffee table out of the way. "Tell me, or tell the cops, I don't give a shit."

He flattened out on the floor, and his eyes narrowed. "You're dead. Your chick's dead too. You got friends, they're dead."

I kept my voice level and said, "Tell me about Harvey Blackstone."

He didn't say anything. I heard a footstep on the deck and took a step so I covered the glass slider with the gun. Joe Mariosa stepped into the room and raised his hands above his head.

"Don't shoot, *amigo*."

I fixed all my attention back on Varega and said, "You followed him from Boston?"

"He made the mistake of trying to pick up his mail." Mariosa smiled and took a 9-mm semiautomatic handgun out of a shoulder holster. "Hello, Jorge," he said. "Long time no see."

Varega said to him, "You're dead," and something else in Spanish I didn't understand.

Mariosa stopped smiling. "I'll take over from here, Mallory," he said.

"You got backup?"

"I want this guy for myself. We have a few old scores to settle."

"That's stupid."

"Maybe. I got a message for you from Mangenello. A Judge Chapman is dead."

My heart sank. I looked at Varega, but he hadn't responded in any particular way to the news—just lay there looking evil while a little stream of blood rolled off the bridge of his nose and down his cheek. I said, "What happened?"

"Don't know. Mangenello wants you to call in."

I stuck the gun in my belt. "I haven't searched him for weapons," I told Mariosa. "Just keep an eye on him while I call. Remember, we want him alive and able to talk." I headed for the bedroom.

I sat on the edge of the bed by the collection of Thoreau's *Journals* and tried to reach Mangenello. They put me on hold. I heard a strangled sound from the front room and shouted through the open door, "Mariosa?"

No answer. I dropped the phone and dove for the other side of the bed as a shot went off behind me. The telephone blew up as the slug hit it, I landed flat on the floor, got the gun out, twisted to see under the bed to the door. I saw Varega's boots and cut loose with two rounds, hitting the door jamb. He jumped back out of sight. I rolled away from the bed, getting behind the heavy oak bureau against the opposite wall. I waited two minutes, then moved to the hallway, bringing the gun up as I made the turn out the door. Nobody.

I inched forward to where I could see into the front room. Mariosa was stretched out on the floor about ten feet away. His eyes were closed, but he was breathing. Bringing the gun out in front of me in a two-hand grip, I did a running roll into the living room—waiting for the sound of Varega's gun. There was nobody but Mariosa.

I checked the pulse in his neck, keeping my head up and the gun pointed halfway between the two entrances to the room. The pulse was steady, and I left him to check the hall to the kitchen. Nobody. Nobody out on the deck either. The Mercedes was still in the driveway, blocked at the road by Mariosa's blue Plymouth.

I looked over the railing at the edge of the precipice. There was a slowing avalanche of loose sand that marked Varega's long slide down the face of the dune. He was a small figure disappearing down the beach toward the south, past the crowds of sunbathers. A few people directly below were looking up from their books, watching me. I shoved the gun into my pants, went back to Mariosa.

He was awake, and he looked up at me as a spasm of pain hit. He forced the words out through clenched teeth, "He had a knife in his boot. Must have palmed it, then stuck me . . ."

"Don't talk," I said. I pulled away his shirt and saw the entrance wound, just below the rib cage.

"Must have nicked a lung," Mariosa said. "Feels real hot inside."

"Hang on. I'll get help."

The phone Jorge had shot was the only one in the house. I went back to the kitchen, grabbed the notebook, then beat it down the stairs to where I'd left the Rambler. It churned up loose gravel all the way out to the highway. There was a pay phone in the parking lot of a convenience store not far from the turn-off for Cooper Road. A police cruiser was parked in the lot, watching traffic coming from Provincetown.

If I went up to the cop and gave him my story, not only would he waste time getting the facts and checking my bona fides before he'd get around to calling an ambulance for Mariosa, but then I'd be in custody. So I used the pay phone. I told the 911 clerk about Mariosa and the location of the house. She tried to interrupt with questions, but I kept talking, giving a description of Varega, telling her he was wanted by DEA, and if they jumped they could catch him before he got off the Cape. When I'd finished I said, "Got that?" If she hadn't, it would be on tape. She asked who I was again, and I hung up.

I waited in the Rambler just sixty-five seconds before the cop in the cruiser picked up his radio handset. He said something into the mike, dropped it, hit his lights, and took off. I was out on the main road when the ambulance came racing past from the opposite direction, headed for Prescott Farm.

CHAPTER TWENTY

Cats

By the time I got to the canal the approaches to the bridge were lit up with flashing blue lights. The cops were checking every car coming off the Cape, looking for Varega. A big trooper at the side of the road waved me over, leaned to window level, then waved me on with a gruff "Routine check" in response to the standard question, "What's going on, Officer?"

I stopped at a fast food place on the other side of the bridge and used my credit card to call Dana, first at home, then at the courthouse. There was no answer at either place. Next I tried Della for messages. My heart jumped when the Judge's voice came over the line. He said "Mallory," in a gravelly whisper, then I heard him gasp for air and there was silence for half a minute. He tried again, but couldn't make the words come. I could tell from the sounds that he was in pain and had to force myself to go on listening. There was a sharp noise, as if the phone had dropped onto a hard surface. I listened until Della's tape ran out, stood in the booth sweating, and took a full minute to dial the next number. Mangenello answered on the first ring.

"It's Mallory," I said, taking a deep breath.

"What happened? They told me you were on the line an hour ago, but you hung up."

"I'm on the Cape."

"I should've known," he said. "I just got a report from our

unit down there. They've got half the force looking for Varega, the other half looking for an anonymous caller."

"What happened to Judge Chapman?"

"He's dead. Why didn't you tell me he was involved with Eden? What the hell's going on?"

"Was he murdered?"

"Looks like a heart attack. His law clerk found the body and raised a fuss. She had my name, wanted me to get in touch with you."

"Where is she now?"

"I sent her home. What the hell were you and Mariosa doing on the Cape?"

"How is Mariosa?"

"In intensive care. He stayed conscious just long enough to get people after Varega. He'll probably pull through. I want some answers, Mallory."

"The house on the Cape belonged to a guy named Prescott. He was a lawyer at Amory and Harcourt, until he got disbarred for stealing from a client. The client was Harvey Blackstone. Prescott is Jack Eden's real name."

"How do you know that?"

"I'm in a phone booth, Simon. I'll tell you when I get up there"

"I'll be waiting," he said, and hung up. I tried Dana's number again, without luck, so I got in the Rambler and headed north.

Back in the city, I didn't stop to see Mangenello, I drove directly to Charlestown. She must have been watching for me. She buzzed open the door before I rang and met me halfway down the stairs. When I put my arms around her she said, "It's so awful."

I kept one arm around her and we went up the stairs.

* * *

"It's my fault," Dana said. "George was here this morning, he found your jacket and went through the pockets and got the picture of Jack Prescott. But on the back it said Jack Eden—the man you'd told me about."

"Prescott is Eden," I said.

She nodded distractedly. "George stared at the picture, wouldn't say anything to me, just dropped it on the floor and walked out."

"Eden was his client."

She wiped her eyes with the back of one hand. "Is that why you've been seeing me, James? To get to George?"

"We can talk about it later. What happened next?"

"You weren't home. I called the Judge. He reacted to the name 'Jack Eden' like Eden was some kind of devil. He hung up, and his line stayed busy for over an hour. I went down to the court and found him."

"And you called Mangenello," I said.

"What did Jack Eden's name mean to the Judge?"

I told her. "The Judge must have done a title search and run across Eden's name on the deeds along with Ben's. Maybe he thought Eden was involved in Ben's murder, but he couldn't say anything without letting people know Ben was stealing land from his neighbors."

"Then he found out Eden was Prescott, a man who hated him. Prescott must have murdered Ben."

"Maybe. I'm going to find out."

"Take me with you."

"I have to see Mangenello first. There's a seven o'clock Delta flight to Bangor from Logan. Meet me at the ticket counter."

She kissed me at the door. I was down to the first floor when her voice came from the upper landing. "Be careful," she called.

The report from the Cape came in as I finished telling Simon everything I was going to tell him. Varega hadn't tried for the bridges. He'd made it to Provincetown in a stolen car, found a small cabin cruiser tied up at one of the marinas with its diesels idling. The owner was waiting for his wife to pick up a few supplies at the marina's grocery. Varega bashed in his head and took off in the boat. It was named the *True Love*. The old guy died in the ambulance on the way to the hospital.

It was late afternoon when I drove down Commonwealth to my apartment. I'd left the leather-bound volume chronicling Blackstone's tax fraud with Simon, but I hadn't told him about the phone call from Jay. If DEA thought Eden was in Sangerville, they'd charge up there to grab him, and no one would take the trouble to unravel his involvement in Ben's death. That wouldn't help Hank.

I had my bag packed and was on my way out the door when I heard sirens on the street. From my front window I saw the fire trucks headed up Mass. Ave. and, over the tops of the buildings across the way, a column of black smoke rising from the South End.

I called Barbi, didn't get an answer. Five minutes later I was downstairs, in the Rambler, out into the rush of traffic on Mass. Ave. The smoke rose from behind the Christian Science center. The corner at Eden's Garden was crowded with fire trucks, hoses, emergency vehicles, and spectators.

It wasn't Mary's building. It was Fred the taxi driver's. As I pushed through the crowd the firemen got a water gun going at the top of a hydraulic lift, and a thousand barrels of city water descended onto what had once been the roof of the building. A cloud of steam gushed up with a roar, the windows at the top blew out, and the crowd murmured with satisfaction.

I found my way through to a red station wagon, where a man in official blue blazer and knee-high yellow boots stood watching the flames. I told him about Fred. "There's no way anybody's coming out of there now," he said. "But there wasn't a cab parked in the alley, so maybe he was on duty."

I left him gazing into the flames and used my key to get into Mary's house to call City Line Taxi. I know the dispatcher, Charlie Smith. I once helped one of his drivers beat a frame set up by a bad cop, and Charlie's still grateful. I asked him to patch me in to Fred's cab. He didn't ask for an explanation, just went off the line for two minutes. When he came back he said, "Can't raise him."

"Keep trying. Tell him his house is burning."

I hung up and rang Barbi, and this time she answered, but my heart sank when she said, "Have you heard from Mary?"

"What happened?"

"She left at ten this morning, while I was in at the Trojan. The cleaning lady was here when a cab showed up and got her. It wasn't duress—she took all her things."

"What cab company?"

"The cleaning lady didn't remember."

"I'll let you know," I said, and rang off.

I rang Michael's house in Hamilton. He was out at the Bombay, but the maid told me she hadn't heard anything about Mary. I tried Caroline, but got no answer.

I ran back to the Rambler and drove down Columbus, checking the sidewalks for Mary's figure, all the way down to Charles Street, past the Trojan, to the Public Garden. I was hoping to find her at the duck pond, dispensing Wonder Bread to the ducks. But she wasn't there.

Back in the South End, the fire department had the blaze under control, but the building was a wreck. The water gun on the hydraulic lift had been turned to wet down the neighboring houses, and a cop tried to stop me from going back into Mary's. I ignored him.

I hadn't checked the upstairs, so I ran up there and went through Mary's bedroom. I went across to the room in front, tearing throw sheets off the furniture, but there was nothing. On the next flight up there were more rooms with old furniture under sheets, but no Mary.

Downstairs in the kitchen I stood to think, staring out through the window at the back. Something was wrong, but I couldn't put my finger on it. The alley and the cedar decks of the next block were obscured by white smoke from the steaming fire, then a gust of wind took the smoke away, and I saw people standing on the decks. The fire had made them neighbors. I looked around the kitchen and realized what was wrong. "Cats," I said out loud. There were no cats. Mary had been there and taken the cats.

I went back out to the Rambler. I could see the tall downtown buildings rising at the end of the street. A storm front had swept over that part of the city, darkening the sky, threatening rain. That's when Matthew, Harvey Blackstone's thug, stepped from behind a parked car and pointed a gun at me.

CHAPTER TWENTY-ONE

Sailing
Sailing . . .

MATTHEW TOLD ME to take Storrow Drive to the expressway and exit at Commercial Street. We made the swing around the waterfront where Dana and I had walked a few nights earlier, then parked in a towaway zone across from the marina where Blackstone kept his boat. The storm front had covered the last of the blue sky to the west, and a stiff breeze blew off the harbor. It looked like an old-fashioned nor'easter was kicking up.

"Careful," Matthew said. "I've got a silencer on the gun, and I wouldn't mind using it. You're going for a sail."

"I've got a plane to catch at seven," I said.

He laughed uneasily. "Shut up and get out of the car."

He followed me out as I stepped onto the pavement, the gun concealed under a leather jacket draped over his arm. "Across the street and down to the boatyard," he said.

As we crossed Commercial Street a few raindrops dampened the blacktop. Blackstone waited for us on the dock, wearing bright-yellow rain gear. As we approached, I watched him cast off the bow line, jump lightly aboard, and sit at the helm. The rain came down in a drizzle. The marina was deserted.

Matthew stayed far enough back so I had no chance to get to him without risking a bullet. We went through the swinging gate to the dock and stepped out onto the slip alongside the *Blackstone III*, a single-masted, forty-four-foot sloop. The inboard diesel engine idled quietly at the stern, bubbling the oily, rain-spattered water.

Blackstone had his own gun, which he held by his side, pointed up at me.

"Permission to come aboard?" I said.

He smirked and lifted the gun a notch. "By all means, Mr. Mallory. It's time for a little talk. George Amory tells me you're stirring up more trouble."

I jumped into the cockpit and stood with the helm between us, close to the gear shift and throttle in the control box by the wheel. I said, "You could have phoned."

He smiled the shark smile. "Cast off the stern line," he said to Matthew.

Matthew stuck the gun in his waistband and put on the leather jacket. He bent to unfasten the cleated stern line. It was tied to release with a quick pull, but Matthew didn't realize that, and he struggled with it. Blackstone took his eyes off me to reach for the end of the line, just as Matthew got it uncleated, and I snapped the gear shift and throttle forward.

The diesel revved into full-throated power, boiling the water against the dock as the boat shot ahead. Matthew grabbed the line and got pulled into the wake. Blackstone looked up to see the bow of his two-hundred-thousand-dollar toy headed straight for a collision with the big pilings twenty yards across the channel. He pulled back the throttle, spun the wheel hard to port. By the time the bow cut sharply out into the channel, churning the stern sideways in a jarring *whack* against the pilings, I had the gun. I braced myself against the turbulence and told Harvey, "Take it on out."

"You're in big trouble," he said.

"I'm in much better shape than I was five minutes ago."

He kept both hands on the wheel, fixing me with an evil,

gloating smile. Out in the harbor there was a slow roll of waves building under the wind, and the spray off the bow mixed with the light rain. As I stepped back to get a grip on the transom, Bill Amory shouted from behind me, "Drop it!"

He must have been waiting in the cabin. Now he leaned out of the forward hatch, a .32 revolver pointed at me. "Drop it and kick it toward Mr. Blackstone." I threw the gun over the side, watched it turn and sink. Amory came crawling down the fiberglass deck, waved the gun to move me into one of the benches in the cockpit, then dropped his legs over and sat across from me.

Blackstone kept the boat on the same heading, out to sea. "Well done," he said.

"Thanks, Harvey," Amory answered. Attorney and client. Amory smiled contentedly, as if holding a gun on the opposing party was the fulfillment of one of his greatest fantasies. "What now?"

"We take him out past the islands, wrap an anchor around him, and let him try to swim home."

Amory stopped smiling. "Wait a minute," he said. "We were going to *talk* to him, maybe hire him to get Varega off our backs."

Harvey glanced up at the blackening sky. With his graying hair and competent hands on the wheel, he looked like a character out of a Hemingway novel. "I've changed my mind, Bill. He's too much trouble."

Despite his sudden discomfiture, Amory kept his eyes on me and held the gun steady. I wasn't convinced he'd shoot, but I didn't want to have any accidents. "That's murder, Harvey," he said, as if informing his client of a minor point of law he shouldn't overlook.

"He knows too much, Bill. If he tells what he knows you're in big trouble. And George. You want George to go to prison?"

"George didn't commit any crime. You and Eden got him into this mess."

I said to Blackstone, "I told the cops everything."

Harvey shrugged. "Maybe. Or maybe you'd say that to save your ass. My guess is you're too independent to turn over evidence to the police."

"Even if I haven't, the police might be your best bet," I said, and turned to look at Amory. "Varega's loose—he knows Eden Development is down the tubes, he'll come after you two. And George."

Harvey and Amory looked at each other, but Harvey shook his head no. Amory brought his eyes back to focus on me. He seemed less sure of himself. The rain was falling steadily now, and Harvey said, "Why don't you give me the gun, Bill, and get yourself some foul-weather gear from below?"

"I'm fine," Amory said.

"How did a respectable attorney like yourself get involved in this mess, anyway?" I asked him, giving my voice an edge of sympathy.

"It was George got us all involved," Harvey answered.

"George had no reason to know there was anything wrong with this deal," Amory said.

"Bullshit. He's in it up to his neck, Bill, and you know it. Why else do you think we gave him a five percent interest in Eden Development?"

Amory's mouth tightened, and Harvey reached casually to turn on the running lights. The compass at the wheel glowed amber. The wind was strong and steady but not yet howling, and the darkness and isolation made the cockpit seem intimate and quiet.

"I fucked up too," Harvey went on. "Should have known dealing with drug money was bad business. But it was such a sweet deal. No bank financing, which meant no accountability, except to deliver the cash to the seller and record the deed. We hold the property for five or six years, sell for maybe twice what we paid, and walk with the cash. When the IRS comes looking, there's nobody there. And the clincher was, Eden needed the local connection and was willing to put up sixty percent of the money for a half share. Plus the deal would be put together by Amory and Harcourt. George really surprised me; he built in some clever safeguards to protect me in case Eden was pulling a con. What could be better?"

"What are you telling him all that for?" Amory said. "You keep talking, we're going to be forced to kill him."

I suddenly realized that was the point. Harvey was buying himself a little insurance.

"Varega showed up a month ago," Harvey went on, as if he hadn't been interrupted. "Came into my office the way you did, Mallory, like a bull in a china shop. Said my original deal with Eden was off. He was taking over and wanted the property sold so he could pull his cash out. He made some threats."

"He couldn't have forced you to sell," Amory said angrily. "He had nothing on paper."

"I wasn't prepared to litigate the matter," Harvey answered him. "I stalled. I told him we'd take a bath if we tried to sell on the present market. And the place was still crawling with low-income tenants—nobody would want to take on that headache." He laughed. "That was a mistake. Next thing I know, he's out there killing people, and we've got lawyers breathing down our necks. Under the scheme we'd laid on for Eden Development, it was a disaster. Hard to keep a low profile when people are dying."

As he talked, I realized George had kept a key element of the deal with Jack Eden a secret—and it was something that would probably upset Harvey. I said, "You're wrong about the cops not having the evidence against you, Harvey. Eden gave it to them."

He smirked in tolerant disbelief. I said to Amory, "Harvey never met Jack Eden? He doesn't know about Prescott?"

Amory said, "Shut up."

"Who the hell is Prescott?"

"A lawyer who stole from you and got disbarred for it," I told him. "Jack Eden is a pseudonym. Eden is Prescott. Varega and this whole mess was Prescott's gift to you."

Harvey's jaw came open, he turned on Amory and said, "Prescott?"

"He's lying!" Amory shouted.

"You son of a bitch. Your sniveling idiot son—"

Amory's face turned red and he swung the gun on Harvey. I said quickly, "Don't blow it now, Bill. Harvey hauled us both out here for one reason—once you'd committed murder together, he'd own you. You'd have to keep your mouth shut, you'd have to fight at his side till the bitter end. All for a lousy tax deal. You and George can give state's evidence and come out fine."

Amory didn't say anything but kept the gun on Harvey, who gave him a look of black contempt and rose out of his seat. With a sudden violence that surprised me, Amory swung his left fist in a sideways swipe that caught his client in the throat. As Harvey went down, the boat swung to port, taking the waves broadside. I snatched the gun, said, "Take the helm, bring us back in." Amory stumbled behind the wheel, pushed Harvey out of the way, cut the wheel to sharpen the arc.

Fifteen minutes later we pulled up to the floating pier at the Boston Sailing Club. "Don't want to go back to the marina," Amory had shouted against the wind a few minutes before. "Matthew," he'd added as explanation. We were suddenly a team.

Harvey sat across from me, one hand at his throat, staring out at the whitecaps blowing off the waves in the harbor. As we bounced against the pier I stood, lifted the gun over my head, threw it into the waves. Amory looked confused and shouted, "Aren't you going to take him in?"

"I've got a plane to catch." I'd given Simon enough evidence for the IRS to nail Harvey. They'd wrap things up without me. And I wanted to get to Eden before he slipped through my fingers.

Amory shouted, "Shouldn't we do something?"

"Do whatever you want," I said, and left them there on the pier. Less than an hour had passed from the time Matthew picked me up on Columbus Avenue until I hopped back in the Rambler and raced through the Calahan Tunnel, out to Logan Airport.

CHAPTER TWENTY-TWO

Back
to Maine

"VAREGA IS HOT," I said to Dana as the plane descended into Bangor International Airport. "He put a DEA agent in the hospital. He can't go back to Boston—probably won't stay in the country. So the people at Eden's Garden will be left alone for a while."

It had been raining when our Delta 707 lifted through the clouds over Boston and raining forty-five minutes later when we finished our drinks and buckled up for the descent. As we came back through the clouds I saw green forests and an occasional lake, washed out silver in the rain. Dana took my hand just before the wheels touched the runway and held it as the plane taxied to the terminal.

An hour earlier I'd run to the boarding gate at Logan and found her trying to convince the flight attendants to hold our plane. They'd hustled us aboard, and once we were airborne I told her about Mary's disappearance and my encounter with Blackstone and Bill Amory. She'd listened without any comment or questions.

We had to wait at the baggage carousel in Bangor, and when Dana's bag came spinning onto the conveyor belt I was surprised to see it was just her briefcase. Then I remembered the gun she had brought on her last trip to Maine, and couldn't have carried onto the plane. I didn't say anything about it. We stopped at the

Avis booth in the terminal and rented a little Chrysler, then headed for Sangerville.

Bangor is the last outpost of civilization before you're lost in the potato fields of Aroostook County. In the last century it was a prosperous lumber and shipbuilding town, but all we saw of it that night was the short stretch of Route 95 before the exit for Route 15. We passed a large and ancient cemetery, half obscured by the rain, and half a dozen big hotels—Ramada, Hilton, Holiday Inn, Budget, Comfort Inn, Best Western.

"What I don't understand," I said, "is why George thought he could trust Eden."

"He probably didn't think it through very well," she said. "George would do anything to impress his father. If Eden had been straight, it could have been a very good business deal." She seemed subdued and troubled, and I wasn't sure whether it was because she was grieving for the Judge or worrying about George.

"When you called last night," she said at last, "I was with him."

"I know."

"I thought you knew, and it made me feel terrible. I told him I wanted to stop seeing him."

"You don't have to explain anything to me, Dana."

"George told Blackstone about finding the picture of Eden in your jacket, didn't he? That's why Blackstone tried to kill you—because of George."

"If he did, he probably didn't think that through very well either."

She shook her head and said, "Poor George."

We got off at our exit, cruised up a hill lined with fast food restaurants, furniture outlets, and a shopping center.

"This is all so crazy," Dana said suddenly. "What does it

have to do with Hank? Eden was after Blackstone, and George, and even the Judge. But why frame Hank for Ben's murder?"

"That's what we're here to find out," I said. "First thing I need is some technical information."

Fortunately there's no shortage of well-stocked hardware stores in northern Maine, even if you're looking for one at eight-thirty on a Saturday night. Coming down a long hill just at the edge of farm country, I spotted a True Value and pulled into the lot. We got wet transferring from the car to the interior of the store. The salesperson on duty was a skinny teenager with long blond hair and pale squinting eyes. He took us to a display of chain saws at the back. "What's the basic principle behind these things?" I asked, giving him the embarrassed grin of a city slicker.

"It's like a bicycle chain, but with teeth," he said, and opened his mouth as if to demonstrate the concept. "Turns on two rotating gears. The power comes from the speed of rotation."

"What if the chain breaks?"

"You replace it. It's not tough." He knelt and showed me the bolts that would have to come off. "A skilled cutter can do it out in the woods with a pair of pliers."

"If you can replace the chain, that means you could take the chain off one saw, put it onto another?"

He stood up and looked at me as if I were crazy. "Sure, you could switch chains on two saws, if they were the same size. Don't see why you'd want to. You interested in buying one?"

"No, but thanks for your help." We hurried back out to the car and started again through the rain. We were on the open road now, with fields and woods off in the darkness at each side.

"Eden switched chains with Hank after the murder, when Hank was milking the cows," Dana said. "When his saw was sitting out in the woods. So it looked like Hank's saw cut the tree that killed Ben."

I nodded. "That still doesn't explain how Eden knew enough about Hank's routine to pull it off."

"Maybe he didn't. Maybe after he'd killed Ben, he came across the saw lying out there and decided to play one of his jokes."

"Quite a coincidence to hit on someone with a motive to kill Ben."

"From what I've heard, that could have been anyone in town."

"Maybe. Next thing we do is stop in Dover-Foxcroft to see Detective Cross."

She said, "Cross was the one who investigated my father's death." At that point the sky really opened up, and I had to focus all my energy on the road, peering through the sheets of water cascading down the windshield.

We made inquiries at the jail and got directed to the local tavern, the Red Oak, where Cross sat at a table eating a late dinner—what looked like three pounds of blood-rare steak and a platter of soggy French fries. The dining area was a little room in the back, dimly lighted by candles set in red water glasses, separated from the bar by swinging, saloon-style doors. A Hank Williams song played on the jukebox next door and a displaced, drunken cowboy crooned along with it.

When we came through the swinging doors Cross glanced up from his food and looked genuinely pleased to see us.

I introduced Dana and he stood up, wiped his hands on a red cloth napkin, reached to give her a handshake.

"You're Judge Chapman's clerk, right? Sorry to hear about

the Judge. He was a fine man. Sit down. Want something to eat?"

"We're on our way out to the Franklins'," I told him. "We'll probably eat out there."

"What are you doing back in this part of the country? Come up to help Jay rescue old Hank? Hank's still out in the woods, you know. Keeps raining like this, he'll float back to town."

"I've got an idea about chain saws."

"Odd thing for a city fellow to think about." He finished chewing a big hunk of steak and put down his fork to listen. After I'd told him he smiled and said, "You done good—got something there for Jay to feed the jury. Won't make McGuire too happy, ruins that open-and-shut case he was so proud of." He winked at Dana. "What's your interest in all this, miss?"

Dana smiled and said, "I'm with Mallory."

He smiled back at her, then stopped smiling and leaned forward a little, as if to see her face better in the dim light.

"What do you know about Jack Eden?" I asked him.

He answered me distractedly, "Fellow from Massachusetts, bought the old Hays place last spring. Haven't seen him since." He turned then and focused on me. "Why?"

"Just curious."

The waitress came in through the swinging doors and started to clear the table, favoring us with a smile as Cross said, "I can't imagine you asking a question without a reason, Mallory. Eden's farm is over on Parkman Road, right by Ben's. You think he's connected to the murder?"

I didn't say anything.

"If you're curious about him, I can take you up there to see his place. Not tonight, the road'll be washed out pretty bad. That'll be all, Betty," he added to the waitress.

When she'd gone I said, "That won't be necessary."

"This is my town, Mallory. I like to know what's going on in it."

Dana said, "Do you remember when Hank's father was killed?"

Cross narrowed his eyes at her. "McOscar," he said. "That's an unusual name. Used to be a McOscar couple spent summers here. Had a skinny little girl."

"That's me," Dana said.

"You've grown up nice. Sure I remember that case."

"Can you tell me a little about it?"

"You writing a book about the rural poor or something?"

"I'm just curious."

He laughed. "Two of you make a pair, full of curiosity. There's still gossip about that murder, even though it happened twenty-five years ago. It's because Ellen Tuttle never spoke a word after it happened, so there was no way to be one hundred percent sure she'd killed Lew. There was even talk that Hank did it, though he was only twelve at the time. He was off in the woods hunting, but he could have come back, caught his old man beating his mom, and put a stop to it. Lew was a wife beater."

"I didn't know that," Dana said.

"Guess he had reason, depending on your attitude about those things. Ellen was what we used to call a loose woman." He hesitated, then said, "I hear the word slut on TV these days, so I guess it's all right to use it in mixed company—and that's a better one to describe her. Slut." He rolled the word off his tongue. "Lew tried to beat it out of her, but that never works." The sudden hostility in Cross's voice had been palpable, and I thought of what he'd told me about his own wife having an affair with Ben Chapman. It hadn't been clear to me whether she'd gone back to him afterward—if she had, I pitied her.

"Maybe she slept around because he beat her, and not vice versa," Dana said.

"Maybe. She was a strange woman."

"In what way, Mr. Cross?"

"Kind of a dreamer. Always reading books."

"Do you think she killed him?"

"I do. There were only two set of prints on that gun—Lew's and Ellen's. Could have been suicide, but Lew wasn't the type. We did have one suspect—man Ellen was supposed to be seeing at the time. You met him, Mallory. Clive Linscott."

I looked up. "What happened with Linscott?"

"Had an alibi. He was on a fishing trip with Ben Chapman, all the way up to Moosehead Lake." He looked a little more closely at Dana and said, "Hank had a baby sister. She'd be about your age now."

Dana got up from the table and went out through the swinging doors. I stood to follow. Cross said, "I'll check out your idea about the chain saw. Should have guessed about your friend, you know. She's the spittin' image of Ellen Tuttle."

Outside the rain had died to a drizzle when I caught up with Dana. She looked at me and said, "Not very nice people, my folks." We didn't say anything more but kept walking. We walked up behind the courthouse into a neighborhood of small houses. I smelled smoke from a wood fire somebody had built against the chill of the rainy night.

"Hank never told you any of that?" I said at last.

"No. Guess he didn't want to remember them that way. Funny, ever since I found out I was adopted, I've had a fantasy about my real mother. Turns out to have been close to the truth." She spoke in a small, calm voice.

"What was the fantasy?"

"When I was a kid, after we moved to Philly, the Judge came down to visit a lot. He always took a big interest in me.

When I found out I was adopted, I decided the Judge was really my father. That Ellen Tuttle had cheated on her husband, that the Judge was her lover."

"Maybe he was."

She frowned. "I don't think the Judge would be lovers with a slut."

"Cross is a bitter old man, Dana. What he said in there isn't necessarily the truth."

We were passing a small, enclosed pasture, and a pony trotted up to the fence and put his nose over to be patted. I heard a car engine and suddenly we were lit up by headlights. I took Dana a step to the side of the road. The horse snorted and took off at a gallop. When the car had passed Dana put her arms around me, then pulled back far enough to see my face. She looked at me solemnly and said, "I'm glad I found you, James Maxfield Mallory."

Then it started to rain again. We made a run for it but were soaked before we got back to the rental car. We turned on the heat and drove out along Main Street, headed for Sam and Jay's.

CHAPTER TWENTY-THREE

God's Little Acre

AT THE FARMHOUSE the fire roared and spit sparks up the chimney, and Sam had set out sandwiches, a silver teapot, four blue china mugs, and a bottle of cognac. Jay convinced me it wouldn't make sense to drive out to Eden's farm in the storm, so after hot showers and a change of clothing, we settled down in front of the fire and talked about Jack Eden, a.k.a. Prescott.

Sam and Jay accepted Dana's presence with the same mixture of intimacy and ambivalence with which they had accepted half a dozen other women I'd brought to visit them over the years. Dana surprised me by telling the story of her parents and of the day Hank Tuttle ran off into the woods with his baby sister—Dana's name had been Judy Tuttle then, the same as Hank's oldest daughter. We talked about the Judge. Sam pointed out that Eden had nailed each of his other victims by turning their own greed or corruption against them, that he had planted the seeds leading to their downfall and settled back to watch his targets do their own cultivating. As I've said, she writes romantic novels and can't always turn it off. "But the Judge wasn't greedy or corrupt," she added. "His weakness was his loyalty to Ben."

It was a good way to spend a cold, stormy night. It occurred to me only once or twice that Hank was outside in the rain somewhere. Then all of a sudden all I wanted to do was sleep.

Dana and I shared the guest room. We had already agreed that the next day I would check out Eden's farm alone. Just before she fell asleep she mumbled, "I wonder if Prescott's here in Sangerville." I lay awake for a long time after that, thinking about Jack Eden.

I woke at dawn, slipped out of bed without waking Dana, and went down to the kitchen. There was coffee in the pot, and I drank a cup with a doughnut before going out to the barn to find Jay. When he saw me he switched off the pump to the milking machines. The cows were stamping against the cement floor, blowing out mist in the cold air, munching at tufts of the hay scattered down the center aisle.

"In Maine you can buy a handgun just by showing your driver's license," he told me, and pulled out a little .32 revolver he'd tucked into his waistband at the back. "Why don't I come with you?"

"Because you might shoot yourself with that damned thing. If I'm not back in two hours, call Cross."

"Why not bring him with you?"

"It'd take too long to explain things to him."

"Go ahead then, do it your way," he said, and smiled. "That's what happens when you listen to too much Sinatra on jukeboxes in sleazy bars. But take the Jeep. You'll need it to get up that hill at Eden's." He looked at his watch. "Two hours is all you get."

Fifteen minutes later I was past the wooden gate at the end of Parkman Road and cruising through a quarter mile of woods lit up red by the early-morning sun. The private road ended at a field that ran uphill to a long ridge. At the crest I could see a house and outbuildings set in a cluster of five big maples. I got the little Minolta binoculars out of the glove compartment and scanned the area between the buildings. Nothing. The road going up had been washed out by the recent rain, but it presented no problems for the four-wheel drive of the Jeep.

I pulled into the yard between the house and the barn and cut the engine. There was sudden, absolute quiet. The top of the ridge was a plateau, a hundred yards wide, dropping off abruptly on the far side, with more fields running down to woods. The view was spectacular. I looked out over two thousand square miles of trees, to Mount Katahdin sixty miles to the northeast, Big Squaw on the shores of Moosehead Lake to the northwest, and a whole range of mountains in between.

It was a very long way from Miami.

I got out of the Jeep and heard a sudden thumping coming from the big old barn across the yard. I went that way cautiously, peered in through the open door. The inside was dark and cathedral-like, lit up by shafts of light that came in from windows high overhead and filtered through a haze of floating dust. It smelled of dust and dry hay. Stalls for horses stood open along both sides of the center aisle, wooden half doors fashioned from hand-hewn boards now gray with age. Overhead the great empty space of the hayloft rattled with the hushed wings of pigeons and swallows. There was a shadowy, canvas-covered mass at the back of the center aisle, and I caught the glint of chrome and a few square feet of blood-red enamel. The thumping started again—a stall door blown by the wind.

Someone had been there before me, fairly recently—a few feet of canvas had been pulled back from the red automobile, and the exposed enamel was only lightly dusted. It was a new Porsche. The odometer said it had traveled just three thousand miles, and it was registered to John Prescott, Fort Lauderdale, Florida. Other than the registration, it was as empty as a car on the showroom floor.

I went back out to the yard. A black crow flew up from one

of the big maples, scolding me as I started across to the house. On the far side of the yard, where it started down the hill, an acre of land had been plowed for a garden. The garden had been left to grow back in weeds, but turning the soil had helped the erosion from the rains, and it was cut by a deep gully running at a diagonal down the hillside. I spotted something in the gulley that made me stop and turn down through the weeds. When I got to what I'd seen, I stopped again and stared at it for a long minute, then said out loud, "Hello, Jack Eden."

It was the partly uncovered torso of a dead man. He'd been wearing a blue T-shirt when he died. It was stained by the earth and what might have been blood. The head and most of the body were still buried in the rich soil of the garden, and I wasn't going to dig it up. But it was clearly a body, and it had to be Jack Eden. It occurred to me I was going to miss the bastard.

And my only hope of getting to the truth now was if Eden had left me some piece of evidence explaining his relationship to Ben Chapman and Hank Tuttle. I went back up the hill, to the house. It had long ago lost its last coat of paint, the long porch sagged, and a parcel post package lay abandoned by the front door. The package was rain-soaked, with a thin green shoot growing out one side, like a stalk from an onion left too long in the refrigerator. The return address on the delivery label said Burpee Seed Company.

The front door wasn't locked. Five of the eight rooms inside were empty. In the kitchen boxes of canned goods had been stacked against the walls, and a few old pots and pans collected mold on top of the woodstove. One of the upstairs rooms must have been used for storage by the antiques dealer who'd owned the place before Eden. It was cluttered with abandoned junk, like a grandmother's attic—an old guitar, beat-up bedroom bureaus, a hat stand with a beret on one of the hooks.

Eden had done most of his living in the big corner parlor downstairs, on the side looking out over the mountains. There was a futon on the floor in front of the large unscreened fireplace, and dozens of books scattered around it. The rest of the floor was crowded with boxes of more volumes, as if Eden had gone to a good used bookstore and bought up their entire inventory.

It was stuffy in the room, I opened a couple of windows and set to work. I was hoping for another phony leather-bound volume, like the one Eden had left for me on Cape Cod. I started with the books lying around the bed. They were heavily marked with underlinings and marginal notes. In a copy of *Walden Pond* I found one sentence underlined twice, with two exclamation points in the margin: ". . . a man is rich in proportion to the number of things which he can afford to let alone." I reflected that Eden had had trouble leaving anything alone. I was kneeling on the floor, paging through a volume of Dickens's *Bleak House*, when I heard a familiar voice from behind me. "What you lookin' for?"

I turned slowly. It was Clive Linscott. He held the big carbine pointed at the floor by my feet, one hand on the barrel, the other at the trigger.

"How'd you know I'd be here?" I said.

"Saw you at the Red Oak last night, talkin' with Cross. I was curious, so I asked Betty and she told me you was comin' out here to check something havin' to do with Ben's murder."

"That's right," I said. "I'm just looking through these books. Maybe you can help."

He frowned and tilted the gun up a notch. "I seen the rain dug up Eden's body, and I seen you find it. I figured someone would find it eventually, but I was hoping it'd be years from now. More's the pity for you."

"I don't know what you're talking about," I said.

He nodded, as if to acknowledge he understood why I was lying. "You're no fool, and neither am I. What you didn't know before, you know now."

I stood slowly, still holding the thick volume of *Bleak House*. "Tell me about it," I said. "Maybe I can help."

He shook his head slightly and shifted his grip on the carbine. "There was a point where a good lawyer could have helped me, but no more. 'Twas an accident, my killing Eden, but nobody would believe it now, and besides, there's other water over the dam. Ben set me up good, but he paid the price. Now you're gonna pay it too, son."

I thought if I threw the book up at his face he might be distracted long enough for me to dive out one of the open windows. Then I remembered how quick he'd been with the gun that day in the woods with Dana, and I looked around for some other way to better the odds in my favor.

"Eden was stealing firewood off one of my lots," Linscott said, with a sudden note of aggrieved innocence. "I come out here to have a few words with him. He was working that foolish garden of his, raking stones from the topsoil. Talked back at me, real wise-ass, and I threw a punch at him. He fell back, hit his head onto a rock, and started thrashing about like something had broke inside his skull. When he stopped thrashing his tongue was stuck out, and he wasn't breathing."

"It was self-defense," I told him. "Then you panicked and buried the body."

"Worse than that. I got scared and just took off. Trouble was, I'd been down to the Red Oak, tellin' folks I was on my way out to give this city fellow a taste of country justice. I thought it through when I got home and came back, but Eden wasn't there no more. I figured maybe he'd come to, that he wasn't dead after all.

"Then I got the call from Ben. He'd been out huntin', seen

me knock Eden flat. Said he'd done me a favor and buried the body but it was in a real shallow grave and someone might stumble on it and remember me mouthing off about him. What Ben wanted was another big chunk of my land. What he got was six feet of God's earth."

He said that with a disturbing note of finality and raised the gun another notch. I said, "Ben did the same thing to you twenty-five years ago, didn't he? When you killed Hank's father."

It was a shot in the dark, but Linscott gave me a startled look, as if maybe I'd been put on the earth to punish him for his sins. "What are you talking about?" he said.

"You deeded that woodlot over to Ben," I told him, "just after Hank's father was killed. And Ben told the cops you were up on Moosehead at the time, fishing." He stared at me with his mouth open. I shifted my feet, getting ready to rush him. "It was fitting," I added, "to kill Ben with a tree he stole from you."

Then his eyes narrowed, and he smiled slyly. "I thought so too. Don't know how you found out about Lew Tuttle, but that was an accident, just like with Eden. He caught me with Ellen and come after me with a gun. We wrestled for it, and he got shot. I run that time too. When I heard Ellen had killed herself, I felt real bad, but didn't see no reason to come forward."

"How'd Ben find out?"

"He guessed. He was my friend at the time. Even offered me an alibi. Should've known I'd have to pay dear for it."

"Why'd you frame Hank for Ben's murder?"

"He'd been talkin' about stirring up things, had the notion somebody here in town killed his old man, and even got that fool McGuire interested. I figured I might as well kill two birds with one stone."

He'd come to the end of the story. "Now we're gonna take a walk out to that garden," he said, "and finish up what I got to do."

What he had to do didn't seem to distress him. Once he had

me out in the open, I wouldn't stand a chance against the rifle. I tried to think of something else to keep him talking until I'd figured some way to get the gun away. I heard the crow scolding outside and a creak of boards on the porch. Linscott heard it too, spun around to cover the window. Dana's face appeared in the opening. Linscott shouted, "Ellen!" and brought the gun up to shoot. I still had the heavy book. I hurled it, catching the barrel on its side as it went off, at the same time diving for him. But I was too far away. He brought the gun back to bear on me, just as Dana leveled her .38-caliber revolver in a two-hand grip and put a bullet into Clive Linscott's head.

Epilogue

DANA HAD WORRIED about me after Jay told her I'd gone off without a gun, and she'd finally decided to ignore our agreement and drive out to Eden's farm. The rental car hadn't made it up the hill, so she'd come in on foot, heard the tail end of my conversation with Linscott, and realized I was in trouble.

Cross showed up twenty minutes later and took us both into custody. It took two full days after that to convince District Attorney Gary McGuire that we'd killed Linscott in self-defense. I spent the time in a cell at the Piscataquis County Jail. While I was there, Jay worked out a deal with McGuire—if Hank turned himself in, he wouldn't be prosecuted for escape. So on the second day Hank joined me in the cell. We played gin rummy, waiting for the forces of law to sift through the evidence, until I was a hundred dollars in the hole and decided to quit playing gin.

In the end, it was Michael Garrison who rescued us. The attorney general for the State of Maine had been Michael's roommate at Choate. He reviewed the case, made one short, angry call to McGuire, and we were free.

As soon as we were released Hank went back to tending the cows. They were going to be his cows pretty soon—Jay had been working on other deals. Hank was suing Linscott's estate for false arrest. With no living heirs but the state, Jay expected a settlement involving a transfer of land and maybe some cash.

Sam and Jay had already agreed to sell Hank the Jerseys, on a no-money-down basis.

Dana spent her two days of captivity in the jail in Bangor, since Piscataquis didn't have facilities for women. Cross, who was happy as a clam over McGuire's discomfiture, insisted on taking me in his cruiser to pick her up, then drove us back to Sangerville with the blue lights flashing. Dana spent that afternoon with Hank in the woods, helping stack cordwood. She never told me all the details of their conversation, but the gist of it was, she had a big brother again.

The unpropertied were cleaning up on other fronts. Two hours after my release I was on the phone to Michael. He had Phil Levine in his office. Phil seemed to get a kick out of talking into Michael's conference speakers. "The IRS works fast," he said. "Eden's property is going up on the auction block, and I'm negotiating to buy the buildings through a nonprofit organization funded by the Commonwealth. My clients thank you," he added. "We're going to have enough funds to complete the renovation, and we're keeping the name Eden's Garden. It'll be a different kind of paradise." I could picture him looking out Michael's floor-to-ceiling windows and smiling.

"Blackstone's got himself hidden behind a screen of good defense lawyers," Michael added, "but with that notebook of evidence against him, he's bound to spend time in jail—or at least pay a big penalty. They might even nail him for the murder of that old guy Solano beat to death."

"What about George Amory?"

"They've got him under wraps, but I assume he's giving state's evidence. Bill Amory will pull off some kind of deal for immunity—he's a fond believer in that old principle of law, 'when the shit hits the fan, make sure it's your client who goes to jail and not you.'"

"The bar overseers will nail them anyway," Levine said.
Maybe, I thought.

My next call was to Simon Mangenello. Varega had never
resurfaced, but the wreck of the *True Love* had washed up on the
rocky coast just south of Plymouth Plantation. The storm that had
hit the Northeast on the night Dana and I flew to Bangor had been
a gale out in the Atlantic. Varega was missing and presumed
dead, which didn't stop Mariosa from climbing out of his hospital
bed to spend a month in the back alleys of Miami and Bogotá,
just to make sure.

I admit to a similar unease about the death of Jorge Varega.
Occasionally I have a dream where I'm lying on the beach at
Cape Cod, reading the latest Judith Krantz, and as I turn to the
last page Varega climbs out of the sea. He points a knife at my
face and says, "You're dead, man."

But I don't have the dream very often.

The next day Dana and I flew back into Logan, got the Rambler from the airport garage, and drove to my office, hoping to
find a letter or a message from Mary Wyman. There was no message on Della, but Edgar was holding a package for me, post-
marked Key West, Florida.

I opened the package very carefully and inside found stacks
of twenty-dollar bills and a four-page letter from Mary.

> Dear Mallory,
> I'm not dead. I've read the newspaper accounts about
> Jack Eden. It's a local story down here, because of the drug
> connection. Thank you for doing such a good job.

I left Barbi's place because I had a dream. I was at the old house. Mother and Jennie were still alive, and I was a child. There'd been a big family party, it was late.

I went out through the front door and down the steps, but instead of the street and the old neighborhood, there were lawns and a forest. I walked barefoot through the wet grass, and then into the forest. I was wearing a white night-dress, like the little girls wear in the china figures Mother collected. The farther I walked, the happier I was.

Some dream, heh? When I woke up, I decided to try to be happy before I died.

I called Fred and he came for me. We stopped at the house for the cats, and took them in the cab to Beacon Hill. That was quite a ride. Nobody was home at Caroline's, but I had a key, and we set the cats free in old Winfred's man-sion. I suspect Caroline has always been more interested in having my cats live with her than having me to take care of—Winfred won't allow pets. I also suspect that once she has a foothold, he won't be able to stop her. Do me a favor, though, check to see that she's treating them well?

After saying good-bye to the cats, we headed south in Fred's cab. I wasn't sure how far I meant to go, but the farther we went, the happier I felt, just like in the dream. We ran out of road in Key West. I've decided to settle here for a while. Hemingway lived in this town many years ago, and raised cats just like me. Their descendants have the run of his old house, which is a museum, and I visit them often.

I think I did the right thing. I just wanted you to know. It's nice and warm down here.

Love, Mary.

Later that day we made a short visit to see Caroline. The cats were all fine, their new mistress sat in a big armchair like a contented Gertrude Stein, and Winfred looked extremely uncomfortable. He told me three times he was allergic to cats.

The cash from Mary added up to slightly more than fifteen thousand dollars. I wasn't sure I had earned it, but I'm not the type to quibble over money. I deposited it in my bank account, hoping the FBI would have fun trying to trace its source.

Then Dana and I headed north for a week of sailing on Moosehead Lake with Sam and Jay. It was early September, the leaves were starting to change, and the evenings were cold—but this time I wasn't sleeping alone. Dana and I were snug in the all-weather sleeping bag on the deck of *Silhouette*. It was another good week.

And then there was Jack Eden. One thing about Linscott's story had bothered me—how had Ben managed to witness Eden's death, realize the potential for blackmail, climb the hill and bury the body, all before Linscott returned to cover his tracks? My questions were answered when they finally dug up the "body" I'd discovered in Eden's garden plot. It turned out to be a shop-window mannequin, probably from the room of abandoned junk upstairs in the farmhouse. The mannequin had been dressed in a pair of Eden's corduroys and the blue T-shirt, which had the face of Henry David Thoreau silk-screened on its front.

Eden's thrashing death in the garden had been another elaborate joke, this time played on Linscott. Eden must have shared the joke with Ben—planting the seeds for Ben's eventual self-destruction, as Sam would say. That didn't stop McGuire from ordering his men to dig up every square inch of that acre of land on the hillside. Of course, they never did find any trace of Jack Eden's body.

But one blustery night in October, after Dana had moved to Philadelphia and I was feeling lonely and restless, I made one more after-hours visit to Security Plus, the private mail box service around the corner from my apartment. Box 331 was still active, the year's fees had been paid in advance, and nobody had bothered to close the account.

I took down the master key and tried the box. Inside was a post card of the Eiffel Tower. The message scrawled on the back read, "Having a wonderful time, wish you were here." It was signed, "Jack."

I decided to follow Thoreau's advice and let it alone. I tacked the post card to the wall over the proprietor's counter, along with the other unclaimed cards, and went back out to the street, locking the door behind me.